ROYAL
A St. Claire Novel

TINA MARTIN

~ . ~

The trueness of love can only be felt.
Not told.
Therefore, one can't simply say
I love you
without expressing that love with actions.

~ . ~

Royal
A St. Claire Novel

Chapter 1

"Royal, get'cho hands off of my butt," Gemma said, standing in front of Royal while they danced to some ol' school music – probably some tunes his father had selected although it could've been Ramsey's idea to play some Teddy Pendergrass. After all, it was *his* party and *his* yacht.

Royal smiled wickedly, causing a muscle in his cheek to flex. "Don't act like you don't like it," he said, biting his lower lip so that his top row of perfectly straight, annoyingly white teeth rested on it.

The gesture made Gemma's heart skip a beat. Why'd she have to be friends with a man so fine? But fine or not, he still needed to remove his hands from her derrière. "I repeat, Royal, get'cho hands off of my butt."

Ignoring her, probably because she'd made

the demand with a smile on her face, he tested his limits by squeezing the plump flesh instead and said, "But I like the feel of this apple bottom. It fits so well in the cradle of my palms."

"Well, we're supposed to be dancing—not bottom-grabbing and grinding."

"Grinding?" he said, raising his brows intuitively. "What do you know about grinding, lil' *innocent*, Gemma?"

She giggled. "Just because I was sick doesn't mean I don't know things. I know what grinding is. It's not something I do, but I know what it is. That's what y'all wild folk usually do to this kind of music, right?"

Royal took Gemma by the hand, spun her around, then settled his hands right back on her bottom. "I wouldn't mind if you decided to get loose and let your boy have a little grind action," he said and had the nerve to gnaw on his lip again. "Gone twerk something, girl."

Gemma laughed. "How the freak am I supposed to twerk to Teddy Pendergrass, *Turn Off the Lights*? Really?"

"You can do it in slow motion," he said flashing a charismatic smile.

Tickled, Gemma said, "You're cute. You really are, Prince Royal, but if you don't keep your hands off of my *apples*, you're going to be dancing by yourself. We already have an audience."

"Who?" he asked, not bothering to look around to see who she was talking about because he didn't care. When he was with her, nothing else mattered and for that reason, he kept his gaze trained on her.

"Your parents, for one. Your mama got her nose turned up like we stank and your daddy looking like he wants to take your place."

Royal laughed.

"And Ramsey's been looking, too, like he's about ready to reprimand you for being so aggressive with me. Ramsey knows I'm a good girl."

"Ramsey also knows every good girl got a lil' freak inside waiting to come out. Why do you think Gianna's pregnant?"

Gemma playfully slapped his arm. "Hush. Don't worry about what married people do. You need to be more concerned about your parents."

"Don't mind them. They've been married since Noah built the ark. I'm sure my dad has done plenty of grinding in his day."

"Then why ain't he tearing up the floor with your mom?"

"I don't know. She's probably not in the mood to dance, or having a case of motion sickness. She does get that from time-to-time, especially on boats." Royal glanced up at his mother and said, "Ooh, she *is* making a stank face at us."

"I told you." Gemma laughed. "So, you need to keep this PG-13," she said, grabbing Royal's arms by the wrist and pulling his hands away from her butt.

"Yes, ma'am," he said, settling his hands at her small waist instead. "Is that better?" he asked, staring at her lips.

"Much better."

As far as Royal was concerned, there wasn't a better way to spend his Saturday – on his brother's yacht, celebrating with the family. His brother Ramsey had married Gemma's sister, Gianna, and they were busy on the dance floor celebrating their marriage and the surprise news that Gianna was pregnant which meant he was due to be an uncle soon. But something else had him feeling like he was on cloud nine on this beautiful day on the open waters of Lake Norman.

It was her.

Gemma.

He moved his hands away from her waist to touch and interlock his hands with hers as they swayed back and forth to the music. Several times, he'd lost himself in the honey color of her eyes and when she'd catch him in a trance, she would only smile – and that smile was equally as beautiful and brilliant as everything else about her. He doubted she knew just how appealing and stunning he found her to be. It didn't matter how much he stared – she hadn't taken the hint.

"Your hands are cold," he told her, staring down at her face. He flirted with the idea of running the pad of his thumb across those beautiful brown freckles on her face and over the softness of her pretty lips. He'd dreamed of kissing those lips and enjoying the warmth of them. The taste of them. For now, he'd keep all of those fantasies at bay and be a friend. That's what she was comfortable with after all. With them being friends. Besides, she was just getting over a sickness. Cancer.

Gemma had surgery about three months ago – a successful surgery, thank God – and Royal, along with Gianna, was there with her in the hospital every step of the way. After Gemma was released, Royal made sure to rearrange his schedule to maximize the amount of time he spent with her. And he kept their relationship at a friendship level ever since, but now standing here staring into her eyes, he knew he couldn't keep up this friendship façade for much longer. He wanted her too much to stay friends. A simple friendship wasn't going to cut it.

Gemma felt him squeeze her hands. She looked up at him and met his glassy gaze. "What?"

"You didn't hear what I just said?" he asked.

"I did. I was ignoring it. I don't need you being my personal thermometer, Royal."

He leaned forward and said, "Sometimes, we need things that we don't know we need." Then he smiled.

Something in her stomach pulled out of nervousness. Maybe it was how close his lips came to her mouth or the brilliance of his smile. Royal had a beautiful smile – no, not beautiful. It was one of those breathtaking ones that made your heart flutter. But everything about him did crazy things to her, and she was sure other women had succumbed to his spell. He was a handsome, six-feet-four, tower of a man. Light skinned with dark black eyes and a beard that plowed into smooth, caramel skin. And he would let her play with his beard. Normally, he wouldn't allow a woman to touch his face, and he'd told her that much, but Gemma had free reign to touch him wherever she wanted and *whenever* she pleased.

"You know I worry about you," he admitted. "Even still."

"Yeah, and I keep telling you...it's not your job, Royal."

"I made it my job, so in a way, it is, beautiful girl."

Gemma blushed.

"And by the way, when I said what I said before, why did you look at me like you didn't believe me?" he asked.

"When you said what?"

"That you looked nice in your outfit. You looked at me like I was lying. Why?"

She shied away from his gaze. She didn't think her outfit was *all that*, especially not attention worthy from a man of his caliber. Since it was an all-white party, she had on a white, fitted dress and a matching white scarf. On her feet were a pair of nude flats. "I honestly think I look a mess," she finally responded. "I was up in the air about coming here."

"Why?" he asked, frowning.

"Because I have to wear this stupid scarf."

"No, you don't. There's nothing wrong with your hair, Gem."

"There is. I don't have any. My hair is still

short. It's just starting to grow back."

"So what?" He shrugged. "It's still pretty. Short hair suits your face. In fact, you can take this scarf off right now," he said, reaching for it.

"No," Gemma said, ducking away from his hand. "Stop it, Royal."

"Okay, okay. Don't panic. Just know that I like your hair."

"Okay. You like my hair," she said. "Noted." She glanced over at Gianna and Ramsey.

Royal also looked in their direction as they danced for a moment, then he returned his attention back to Gemma, his eyes tracing her nose. Outlining her lips. He licked his lips, then asked, "Do you think she's happy?"

Gemma turned her focus back to Royal. "You mean Gianna?"

"Yeah."

"Oh, God yeah." She laughed a little. "She's over the moon. Do you think Ramsey's happy?"

Royal nodded. "I haven't seen him this happy in a long time." Royal released Gemma's hands to position his hands at her waist again while staring into her eyes, feeling her body tremble beneath his touch. Why was she so nervous all of a sudden? She wasn't nervous when he had his hands on her butt or was it the combination of staring into her eyes that had her shook? Nah, he quickly decided. They'd spent so many days together, she had no reason to be uneasy around him. Just last night he was with her for a few hours watching a movie and eating dinner. Now she was nervous?

"Hey, I was thinking...you should probably let Ram and Gianna have the house to themselves tonight," he told her. Gemma had been living with Ramsey and Gianna since the couple married.

"And where am I supposed to stay?" she asked.

"With me," he offered up casually like it hadn't been on his mind the whole time.

Gemma furrowed a brow. "So, I'm supposed to stay in your bachelor pad?"

"Yeah. Why not? You've been to my place before."

"Yeah, only twice and I've never spent the night."

Royal watched a jet boat breeze past them then said, "There's a first time for everything right?"

"Right."

"Besides, I need to talk to you about something."

"Must be important. You've got that serious look on your face."

He softened his features. Smiled at her. "It's something close to me. And, yes, I'll tell you all about it when we get home."

When we get home...

She wondered if he heard what he said and if perhaps he meant to say *when you get to my condo* or *when we leave here*. Instead, he said, *when we get home* like he considered his home to be her home as well. The place where she was supposed to be. Or maybe she was reading too much into it, but something told her she wasn't. She'd noticed that Royal seemed to be getting more and more comfortable touching her lately, but especially so this evening. And she'd caught him several times staring at her with the same intensity that Ramsey had been staring at Gianna for most of the party.

"Why are you so quiet, Gemma?" he asked.

She glanced at the hair beneath his bottom lip when she responded, "No reason. I'm just enjoying this—the wind brushing against my cheeks and being out here with the family. The love in the air feels so electrifying."

You have no idea, he thought.

"This is my first time on a boat," she told him.

"I know."

"And I've never danced with a prince before," she quipped.

He chuckled. "Well, this is my first time dancing with a princess." *My princess.*

Gemma cackled. "Oh please, Royal. I see some beautiful woman checking you out whenever we're together. I know you've dated some *princesses* in your day."

"Just because a woman is beautiful doesn't make her a princess. It's about class. The way she carries herself. The way she treats others."

Gemma nodded, appreciating the fact that a man actually looked beyond the outer layer of a woman to see what she was really made of. She was glad that he was that kind of good-hearted, common sense person. "Hey, I just thought about something. I can't stay with you tonight."

"Why not?" he asked failing at an attempt to

hide a frown because he wanted her to stay with him more than anything.

"I don't have any clothes."

"Nice try, but we're still in Lake Norman. We can swing by Ramsey's and pack an overnight bag for you."

"Oh. Okay, then. Problem solved, I guess."

Royal squeezed her waist again. Licked his lips again, finding it a challenge to take his eyes off of her lips.

"Hey, you know the music just stopped, right?" she asked, looking at him instantly feeling the heat of his eyes on her lips. She moistened them. "Royal?"

"Yes?" he asked, connecting his gaze to hers.

"The music stopped."

"I know."

She chuckled uncomfortably. "Then why are you still cinching my waist?"

He offered up a half shrug. "No reason."

Gemma's cheeks reddened before she wrapped her hands around his wrists moving his hands away from her body for the second time this evening. Feeling like they needed a break because she definitely needed time to maintain a steady heartbeat again, she said, "I'll be back. I'ma go holla at Gianna for a second."

"Okay. Hurry back so I can do some more grabbing."

Gemma stuck her tongue out at him and he pretended to grab it and toss it inside of his mouth, making fake chewing movements. She laughed, then continued walking over to where

Gianna was standing.

All the while, Royal watched every single step she took, eyeing her fit, little body down and secretly rejoicing that he'd have her all to himself tonight. At his crib. In his arms. He could hardly wait.

"Man," Romulus said, stepping up to Royal. "If you stare at her any longer, you'll be able to read her thoughts."

Royal chuckled. "You should know, huh? You've been reading Siderra's for how long now?"

Romulus grinned. "Nah. Me and Derra are just friends. But you—you got a thing for this girl."

Royal looked at the brother that could be considered his twin and said, "You're just now figuring that out, Rom? Me and Gemma have practically spent every day together for the last two-and-a-half months. Yes, I have a thing for her."

"And you haven't made a move yet?" Romulus asked, sliding his hands into his pockets, catching a glimpse of Siderra staring at him and when he caught her gaze, she quickly looked away.

"Nah. Not yet."

"You're losing your touch. You usually move quicker than that don't you, bro?"

"Usually, but not with her. She's different."

"Oh shoot. That's the same nonsense Ramsey was talking when he met Gianna, and they're married."

"Funny how that works, isn't it?" A smile

settled in the corner of Royal's mouth.

"Tell me—what is it that makes Gemma so *different*?" Romulus asked.

Royal glanced over at Gemma again before he responded, "She just is."

Chapter 2

The party was over. Royal and Gemma were among the first to leave since he had to take her home to get clothes. And now, they were on the way to Charlotte – more specifically to Charlotte's Dilworth Neighborhood –near Uptown.

Royal glanced over at Gemma as she sat in the passenger seat of his Tesla. Her eyes were closed, but he knew she wasn't sleeping. He could almost feel it.

"Are you hungry, Gem?" he asked her.

"No. It's late anyway."

He glanced at the clock on the car's touchscreen radio display. "It's nine something."

"Yeah, but I'll get heartburn if I eat a meal this late Royal."

"Right," he said. He knew that. Just like he knew the name of every one of her prescriptions and when she needed to have them refilled. He'd recorded it all in his personal calendar on his cell. And he knew other things about her – like when she needed water. When she was happy or feeling overwhelmed. Right now she was relaxed, yet spent from the party. He'd purposely kept her on the dance floor for as long as he could, intent on showing her a good time.

He glanced over at her again. Her eyes were still closed, displaying the impressive length of her lashes. Her breathing remained gentle. Steady. Ambient light made her cheeks glow and appear soft like he already knew they were. He wondered what was going through her mind? Was she thinking about Gianna? Or maybe Gianna's announcement that she was pregnant? To keep a conversation going, he asked, "How do you feel about being an aunt?"

Gemma opened her eyes and stretched her body while she yawned. "I'm excited. I'm so happy for Gianna. For a while there, I didn't think she would ever find someone."

"Why not?"

Gemma shrugged. "Because she wasn't looking."

"That's usually when you find something...when you're not looking for it." *That's how I found you.* That was the truth. When he volunteered himself to stay with her at the hospital, he had no idea how quickly she would touch his heart.

She smirked then glanced over at him. "If you say so, Royal."

"I know so," he said palming her left thigh, squeezing firmly then letting go when he felt her body jerk.

She cleared her throat and hoped he didn't feel it. This was the second time today she'd had this kind of response to his touch. Why was she so jumpy like Royal's hands had never been on her thigh before? She wasn't the fidgety one. Gianna was.

"Sorry, did I scare you?" Royal asked.

"No. You just—um—sort of caught me off guard. That's all. Now, keep your hands to yourself."

Royal laughed. "You say that now then later it's, *oh, Royal, I'm cold. Can you hold me? Royal, can you rub my back? Royal, I need those strong arms around me*," he teased, trying to imitate her voice when he said it.

Gemma chuckled. "First of all, I've never said *put those strong arms around me*."

"Yes, you have. Stop lying, Gem."

"I haven't," she said, still tickled. "O-M-G, you're full of it, Royal."

He was steadily laughing, cracking himself up.

* * *

When they arrived at his condo, he took the liberty of walking around the car to open the door for her – something he'd always done especially since he still considered her to be in the recovery phase after her surgery. He reached for her hand, then helped her to her tired feet.

"Thank you."

"You're welcome." He handed her the keys and said, "Go ahead and unlock the door. I'll get your bag."

"Okay," Gemma said walking on up toward

the entrance. "I better not walk in and find a naked woman spread eagle on your sofa."

Royal grinned and glanced up at her as she unlocked the door. Then he walked quickly to join her inside of his place. Having her here made his two-bedroom, modern-style decorated condo feel even more like home, adding warmth that was sorely lacking until she showed up. This was her third time here, but the first time she would spend the night.

Gemma slid out of her shoes, leaving them by the door.

"I'll be right back...going to put your bag in the spare bedroom. Make yourself at home."

"Okay." Gemma continued barefoot onto the kitchen where she took a glass from the cupboard and filled it with ice and water.

After leaving her bag on the bed, Royal returned to the open living room – kitchen area and stood there watching her drink water. She was just about to take another drink but as she turned up the glass, she caught his gaze. Smiled.

"What?" she asked, noticing he'd come out of his white jacket, bow tie and had unbuttoned his white shirt three buttons down.

Royal leaned against the wall and eased his hands into his pockets but didn't say a word to answer her. He just observed her in his home. Her presence here felt organic – like she belonged. He had other women over but never one as interesting as her. Maybe it was the fact that she didn't blush around him or wasn't trying to impress him or beautify herself in his presence in hopes of winning his affection and attention. But why would she? After all, they were *just friends* – well friends who were now in-laws since Gemma's sister married his brother.

"Royal?"

He came out of his reverie at the sound of his name off of her lips and smiled big and bright, so much so that Gemma took in the full picture of him standing there thinking that while nobody on earth was perfect, Royal St. Claire came pretty darn close to it. The white clothes he had on enhanced the creamy goodness of his skin. His teeth were straight and as white as his clothes. Eyes, mesmerizingly black, matching the color of his hair. He would alternate styles of wearing a beard, goatee and sometimes he shaved it all off and go with a simple, well-groomed mustache. Whatever he did, it suited him.

"So, what's up?" Gemma asked, feeling her body temperature rise under the spotlight of his gaze, thinking that it was odd for him to be staring at her this way. What was he thinking about? And why was he smiling?

"What's up with you?" he asked.

She threw her head back. "Okay...I thought you had to talk to me about something."

"I do. Do you have the popcorn ready?"

"Popcorn? You didn't say anything about no popcorn."

"I'm saying it now. Pop some."

"And how am I supposed to know where you keep the popcorn?"

He was quiet as he stepped around the counter to the kitchen then over to the pantry. She followed and watched as he opened the door then turned around and looked at her.

Her eyebrows raised. "Oh. You want *me* to reach up there and get it."

He gestured for her to do so.

"What's wrong with your hands?" she asked.

"Nothing. I just want you to know where things are," he told her.

"O-kay..." Gemma stepped in front of him and rose up on her tiptoes to remove a box of Pop Secret from the top shelf. As she did so, Royal, standing behind her, closed his eyes while taking in the scent of her. He didn't know what it was she was wearing, but it smelled heavenly against the fragrance of her own skin.

"You got me reaching up here and you're taller than I am," she told him.

"Really? I hadn't noticed," he joked.

"My point is, it wouldn't have been nothing for you to grab this from the top shelf."

"Yeah, but I wanted you to do it, Gemma."

"Bet you did..." she mumbled while opening the box. She removed one package and tore the plastic wrapper off of it before placing it inside of the microwave. Then she turned around to look at him. He was staring at her again, in an inquisitive way this time she could decipher, and that made her cross her arms over her chest and stare back squinting at him – doing a little examination of her own. "What?"

A weak smile grew on his face. "Nothing."

"Then why are you staring at me like you

want to say something?"

"Because I *do* want to say something," he said.

"Then say it."

The microwave beeped. Royal took a big, white bowl from one of the lower cabinets and handed it to her.

"Thanks. Now, stop keeping me in suspense. What is it that you have to tell me?"

"Stop being so impatient, woman," he said taking the bag from her. He poured the popcorn into the bowl.

"I wouldn't have to be *impatient* if you would stop keeping me in suspense."

"Oh Gemma, Gemma, Gemma. What am I going to do with you, girl?" He tossed a single popcorn kernel into his mouth.

"Tell me what it is you have to say so I can't move on with my life."

Royal smiled. "Why are you so impatient?"

"Hello!" Gemma said, brightening her eyes. "I almost died, remember? That's why I like to know things. I know how it feels to have no tomorrow."

The smirk fell off of Royal's face. He wanted to tell her not to talk that way, but fearing it would destroy their carefree conversation he resisted. "Grab your water," he told her as he headed to the living room.

She took her glass, filled it back up with tap water then sat a cushion away from him on the sofa. Removing one of the wooden coasters, she placed it on the shiny, wooden table and then set her glass on top of it.

Royal looked at her. "You know I have bottled water in the fridge right?"

"Yeah," she said reaching into the bowl, grabbing a fistful of popcorn then crammed it all into her mouth.

"Gem, if you're hungry—"

"No. This is good," she mumbled with a completely stuffed mouth.

Royal watched her chew. Women he dealt with never did stuff like this – eat recklessly and carefree. Amazingly, he wasn't the least bit turned off by the fact that she ate a handful of popcorn at once or the fact that she was talking to him with a mouth crammed so full, popcorn was falling out. Things that would normally turn him off, she got a pass for.

"I was thinking about everything you had to go through with the surgery and being sick with cancer and all—"

"What do you mean you were *thinking* about it?" she asked, interrupting him.

Royal adjusted his position on the couch angling his body towards her. "Just what I said. I was thinking about it, so much so, that I went to Ram to see if there was a way St. Claire Architects could do something to help people in a similar situation. People who could possibly...um...die if they can't afford treatment."

Gemma shoved another handful of popcorn into her mouth. "What did you come up with?" She glanced up at him to see his eyes on her mouth. She quickly covered her mouth, smiling as she did so, mumbling, "Sorry. I'm not being very *ladylike* am I?"

"I don't care how crazy you're eating. I just want you to pay attention to what I'm saying while you're eating."

"Okay. I am. You said you went to Ramsey to see what the company could do to help people who were in a situation like I was."

"Yes, and I proposed that we come up with a foundation named after you."

Gemma stopped chewing and glanced up at him. "Do what?"

"I want to name it in honor of you."

"Um, hello! I'm not dead."

Royal chuckled at the seriousness of her expression. "You don't have to be dead for someone to honor you, silly."

"But I didn't do anything to deserve this."

"But, nothing. Stop trying to tell me why you don't think you deserve it and tell me how you feel about the idea of it all."

"I—I—" Gemma didn't know what to think. Well, she did but it was so far beyond her wildest imagination to have a foundation named after her that she didn't know how to react to it.

"Gem?"

She glanced up at him and tilted her head to the side. "Whose idea was this? Yours or Ramsey's?"

"What does that matter?"

"I just want to know."

"If you were paying attention to me instead of murdering that popcorn, you would've heard me when I said *I* brought this idea to Ramsey."

She mused over it for a minute and said, "I think it's a good idea. It saved my life so maybe it will save someone else's."

Royal nodded and tossed some popcorn into his mouth.

"It probably shouldn't be named after me, though," Gemma said, rubbing her buttery hands on the pant legs of her white jeans. It's not like she would ever wear them again, anyway.

"Why not?" Royal asked, standing up. He sauntered to the kitchen and returned with a couple sheets of paper towel for her.

"Oh. Thanks," she said.

"You're welcome." He sat down again. "Why shouldn't it be named after you?"

With raised shoulders, she responded, "Because I don't think I did anything to deserve it."

Royal took the bowl from her lap and set it on the table. Then he motioned for her to come closer to him. She did, moving slowly to sit right in the cradle of his pelvis. "Thank you for not squishing my balls this time."

Gemma giggled. "I wouldn't have squished them the last time if they weren't so big."

"Can't argue with you there," Royal said. He circled his arms around her waist and Gemma fell right into his embrace enjoying the feel of his warm, hairy arms against her skin. She recalled how when she first met Royal, she nearly had hot flashes every time their eyes met. That's how handsome he was. But when she knew Royal had no interest in her, her comfort level with him increased day-by-day to what it is now. As far as she was concerned, Royal and his three brothers for that matter, were the brothers she never had – especially Royal. He had stayed with her in the hospital for weeks and didn't know her at the time. But a couple months later, *they* were 'them'. Royal and Gemma. You hardly saw one without seeing the other.

Royal squeezed her into his embrace and let himself feel all the emotions he had for this woman swirling around inside of his mind and heart. For him, their friendship started out as a protective type of relationship. One where he felt the need to safeguard her, even from herself if need be. That desire ballooned into something he hadn't expected – a longing to see her every single day. An inherent need to be close to her. Even in his arms right now she wasn't close enough.

He drew in the thick scent of her sweet fragrance. "I want to name the foundation after you, Gemma, because not only do you represent the type of people were looking to help, but you fought your own battle and won. I'm proud of you for that. You are a strong, beautiful black woman and I truly feel you deserve everything good that's coming to you."

"Wow," she said, picking at his arm hair. "You put it so eloquently."

"It's the way I feel about it." Royal took her small hand into his and stroked his thumb along the back of it down to her wrist. "I'm waiting for you to object. I know you have *something* to say. You always got something to say."

"Nope. Not this time. I'll let you have your way." Gemma smiled, interlocking her fingers with his. "But seriously, thank you for thinking of me."

"I always think of you, Gemma," he said softly, and nothing in him gave him pause about expressing how he felt in that moment.

Gemma could hear and feel the truthfulness of those words as she felt goosebumps consume her entire body. She smiled, touched by his expression. Royal always knew what to say to make her smile. To make her feel good about herself even if it was just fluff or a friend being nice because, well, that's what friends were supposed to do, right?

"Hey, why don't you go get changed so you'll be ready for bed," Royal suggested.

"No. I'm fine right now," she said leaning forward to take the remote off of the table. She powered on the TV and leaned back, reclining against Royal's chest again.

"What are you doing?" he asked.

"Looking for a movie."

"Gemma, go get comfortable. You know, just as well as I do, that you don't stay awake in these arms for too long."

"You think you know me so well," she said, channel surfing.

"After nearly twelve weeks, I don't *think* I know you. I *do* know you. Now go on get changed. And bring your medicine in here, too."

Gemma stretched. "But I don't want to get up. I'm nice and comfy."

"Then hurry up and change and you'll be back comfy in no time."

She sat up then twisted her body to look at him and frowned.

He smiled. Even her frowns were endearing – as stunning as the features that enhanced her beauty. "Go 'head, Gemma. I'll be here when you get back."

"Ugh..." she said standing. "You get on my nerves."

"Love you, too, bae," he quipped watching as she rolled her eyes. He didn't take his eyes off of her until she was out of sight – when he didn't have much choice. He stretched and draped his long arms around the back of the sofa, exhaling sharply. With his eyes closed, he took a moment to relax, tired from a long day of partying but genuinely happy for Ramsey. His brother had found love again – something the family never thought he would do.

"Sleepy?" Gemma asked.

Royal opened his eyes the moment he heard her voice and saw her standing in a white T-shirt-style nightgown that read in bold letters: **Namaste In Bed**. He cracked a smile then studied her skinny legs down to her small feet before returning his attention back to her face. She'd also taken off the white scarf she had on and used a black scarf to secure her hair.

"You got your pills?" he asked.

"I took them already," she told him. "Hey, it's late, Royal. Why don't you go ahead and go to bed? I know you're just as tired as I am."

"I am tired, but I want you right here."

"Royal, go to bed. Wouldn't you be more comfortable in—"

"If you don't bring your butt over here, I'm coming after you."

She smiled small then it grew. In her mind, she could picture Royal chasing her around the coffee table.

"That's what you want, isn't it?" he asked moving to get off of the sofa.

"No. I'm coming," she said walking over to him, then easing back into his lap cradling her body into the mold of his.

"Perfect," he said after she got comfortable. "Now, let me get this scarf off of your head."

"Touch my scarf and you die," she told him.

Royal chuckled. "I don't know why you make such a big deal out of that."

"Because it's *my* scarf, and it's *my* head. I don't tell you what to do with your hair. One day you're smooth shaven and the next, you look like Wolverine."

Royal laughed. "You are something else. You know you're the only person who talks to me this way."

"What way is that?"

He shrugged. "Like you're not afraid of me."

"I'm not afraid of you."

"Okay, maybe *afraid* is the wrong word. I don't want you to be afraid of me. I want you to be exactly who you are. A super sweet, smart-mouthed lil' thang."

"Now *that* I can do," she said absentmindedly threading her hand with his again. Not only had she grown comfortable with Royal's affable nature, but she also trusted him too – odd because the only person she trusted was Gianna. And she'd never been close to a man. Especially one so devastatingly handsome, smart and *alpha* like Royal. Yet she melted into his arms like marshmallows in hot butter.

Royal listened as she inhaled a deep breath and let it out evenly. She was probably unaware of her pre-sleep techniques but he knew them well. Knew her well. Within minutes she'd be asleep, in his arms – just the way he wanted it. When he felt the grip she had on his hand loosen, he smiled then whispered, "Goodnight, Gemma."

On the verge of sleep himself, he yawned and stretched a little so as not to disturb sleeping beauty then picked up his cell from the table next to the sofa. He saw a missed call from Ramsey thirty minutes ago. He immediately dialed him back.

"Royal, where's Gemma?" That's how Ramsey answered the call.

"I got her," Royal told him.

"You *got* her."

"Yeah...right here in my arms. She's sleeping."

"Gemma's spending the night with you?"

"Yeah. I figured you and *cupcake* could use some privacy."

Ramsey grinned. "I have a separated, third-story suite. We have plenty of privacy while

Gemma's here."

"You could just say thank you, Ram."

"For what? I told you Gemma is no bother to us. We have privacy with her around. I have a live-in butler, remember? Carson? So, tell me— what's the real reason you decided to take her home? I saw you all up on her at the party."

Royal pressed his lips at the top of Gemma's scarf-covered head and then said evenly, "Okay, maybe I wanted her here with me."

"Now, we're getting to the truth of the matter," Ramsey said. "There better not be no funny business going on over there either."

Royal shook his head thinking that his brother was just as intrusive as he was bossy. "I see Gianna is rubbing off on you. Sounds like something she'd say," Royal told him. "And I told you Gemma's sleeping right now."

"Well, feel free to bring her home tomorrow. Gianna will be worried sick if you don't and I don't want any stress on my wife."

"Gianna knows Gemma is in good hands with me, and if she doesn't know, have her call me in the morning. I'm keeping Gemma for the weekend."

"Keeping her for the weekend?" Ramsey repeated. "You say that like she's yours."

"She *is* mine."

"Whoa...really? That's how you feel?" Ramsey asked.

"Yeah. That's how I feel. I'll talk to you about it later. I'm going to put Gemma to bed right now. And don't mention anything to Gianna about, you know..."

Ramsey chuckled. "Anybody with eyes can already see it, Royal."

"Not necessarily," Royal told him. "Gemma has eyes. She can't see it."

"You don't think she has a clue that you're feeling her when literally you were feeling her up on the boat?" Ramsey inquired.

"Not one clue. To her, I'm just a friend."

"What are you going to do about it?"

"Not sure yet. I've never been in the friend zone before, so I'm not sure how to work my way out of it. Anyway, I'm going to get her to bed. I'll holla at you on Monday."

"Alright, man. Take care of my sister-in-law."

"Yep," Royal said, then hung up the phone and shifted his body a little to make Gemma more comfortable. He grabbed a piece of cover that he kept tossed across the sofa and spread it over her. Then he laid back staring up at the ceiling and said softly, "Everybody can see it except you, Gemma."

Chapter 3

In the morning, Gemma woke up in the guest bedroom. After a quick bathroom visit, she dialed Gianna's number while lazily walking down the hallway toward the kitchen. She smelled food, so she assumed Royal was in there.

"Hey, are you on your way back?" she heard Gianna ask.

"Good morning to you too, sunshine," Gemma quipped. "How are you doing Gianna?"

"I'll be doing a lot better when you get your frisky tail home."

Gemma grinned. "Did you say frisky?" She laughed some more. "Who says frisky?"

"Well, just get your butt back to this house. How about that?"

"Why are you being so mean?" she asked, but she already knew Gianna wasn't necessarily a morning person. In fact, she wished she'd waited until the afternoon to call her. She would've been fully awake by then. More rational.

"Gemma don't make me come to Charlotte and pick you up myself."

"Okay, now you're going—" Gemma's voice

caught in her throat when she saw Royal sitting on a barstool at the small island countertop in the kitchen. Shirtless. What was he trying to do? Make her heart completely stop first thing in the morning? *Good Lawd!*

"Hello?" Gianna asked. "You there?"

"Um—" Gemma couldn't find words as she stared at the sculpted perfection of this man's chest. What? How? Was this real? She thought men's bodies only looked like this in movies.

Royal looked up from his tablet and focused his attention on her. Since she was on the phone, he opted to wave by throwing up his right hand just barely, and even that looked cool and sexy.

Gemma didn't wave back. How could she wave? Oxygen wasn't getting to her brain and since it lacked oxygen, her brain wasn't functioning properly. Since it wasn't functioning, how could it tell her to move her arm? Seeing Royal with his shirt off nearly made her lose her footing and her thinking ability. Wow!

"Gemma?"

Gemma blinked when she heard Gianna's voice. She'd momentarily forgotten she was on the phone. Finally coming out of her trance with Royal – more like coming out of a trance with Royal's body – she said, "Uh...umm...I forgot what I was saying," she admitted.

Royal smirked then resumed his business on the tablet.

"Okay. That's it. I'm coming to get you," Gianna said.

"Gianna, I'm fine. Royal's not going to harm me. You act like he's a danger to me," she said glancing up at Royal, meeting his gaze. He looked to be interested in the conversation now since hearing his name.

"I know he's not a danger to you, but he's a *man* and if he's as charming as his brother—" Gianna paused and said, "You know what...put him on the phone."

"Oh, jeez. Hold on." She placed the call on mute, then said to Royal, "My *smother* wants to talk to you."

He laughed, then said, "I'm in a world of trouble now, huh?" He took Gemma's cell phone, pressed the mute button to turn it off, then said, "Good morning my dearest sister-in-law."

"Don't even try to sweet-talk me. Why did you take my sister?"

Royal chuckled. "You make it sound like I kidnapped her or something."

Gemma shook her head wordlessly.

"You may as well have. One minute, you had her detained on the boat. The next, y'all gone."

"Did you say I had her *detained*?" Royal laughed.

"Yeah, and don't try to play dumb. You know exactly what I'm talking about."

"Okay, look, Gemma. I thought I told you Gemma was going to be with me."

"I don't recall you telling me anything like that."

"Well, I apologize. That's my bad. I just thought it would be a good idea for her to stay with me this weekend."

"And what made you think that?"

"It was my way of stepping in to give you and Ram some alone time and—"

"My sister is not a bother to me."

"I know that Gianna, but trust me when I say she is fine."

Gianna sighed heavily. "Did she take her medicine last night?"

"She did."

"This morning?"

"She's about to."

"And what about food? Has she eaten? Do you even know what she can and can't eat?" Gianna asked.

"I do. She doesn't eat spicy foods and she doesn't eat late to avoid getting heartburn. I got this, Gianna. I was in the hospital with Gemma, remember? I know about her care and I know how to take care of her," he said glancing up at Gemma, catching her eyes on his chest.

"When are you dropping her off?"

"Tonight, maybe. I'm not sure yet."

"Okay. Put her back on the phone, please."

"Yes, ma'am." Royal pretended to wipe sweat from his forehead and handed Gemma the phone across the table.

"Have you calmed down yet, sis?" Gemma asked her.

"Yeah. I feel a little better now. Just take care of yourself."

"I will, Gianna. Why do you sound so sad?"

"I'm not sad. I just worry about you. That's all."

"I'm fine. I promise. I'm with the prince." She glanced up at Royal and winked. He winked back.

"Okay. Just make sure *the prince* keeps his hands to himself."

"What?" Gemma asked laughing. "You said...make sure..." Gemma laughed harder –so tickled that she couldn't get the rest of it out. "I know *that's* not what you're worried about, and if you are, let me assure you...it ain't *that* kind of party, Gianna."

"Okay. If you say so. I love you, sis. See you tonight."

"Love you, too, Gianna. Bye."

Gemma was still grinning when she hung up the phone.

"What's got you so tickled?" Royal asked before he pressed something on his tablet then pushed it aside on the granite countertop to give Gemma his undivided attention.

"Nothing," she said, but she found it hilarious that Gianna thought Royal had the slightest interest in her. Let Gianna tell it and Royal was in love with Gemma, trying to charm her into his bed or something. She found the notion comical. Royal wasn't checking for her like that. Why would her sister think such a thing? Because that's what Ramsey did to her?

"So, being that I woke up in the middle of the guest bed, you must have taken me in there because I don't remember a thing."

"Yep, I took you in there. You fell asleep in my arms on the sofa last night. I fell asleep, too. When I woke up, you were still sleeping like a baby, so I put you in there on the bed. How did you sleep by the way?"

She glanced at his chest again and said, "Beautiful. I mean, good. I slept good."

"Sure about that?"

"Yeah. Why do you ask?"

"Because you tossed and turned a lot."

She frowned. "How do you know that?"

"Because I watched you for a while."

"You're funny." Gemma laughed. He actually said that with a straight face. "Anyway, where are your clothes?"

Royal looked down at his bare chest then back up at her. "So you slept okay?" he asked again.

"I did, and I don't know if you're joking about watching me sleep or what, but I did sleep okay. I usually toss and turn in my sleep. It's completely normal. Nothing to be alarmed about."

"That's good to know, and no I wasn't joking. I watched you."

Her smile faded when she noted he was serious. When she saw the muscles in his jaw clench. "That's a bit intrusive, don't you think?"

"No, I don't," he said. Like Ramsey, she noticed that Royal liked joking around from time-to-time but he had a serious side, too. "I made you some oatmeal for breakfast," he said standing up, walking to the microwave. While he walked, Gemma tried not to stare at his smooth complexion, the muscle definition in his back and arms and just the overall way he was beautifully built. And those sweatpants he had on hung right off of a tight, steel butt and when he turned around to walk back toward her, she checked out the front. The man had muscles for days – abs that should've been outlawed and a sculpted Adonis belt that lead down to what had to have been something impressive beneath those pants. She chewed on her lip thinking about what a woman must have felt being made love to by a man like him and ways he could move his body and tempt a woman just by looking at her with his determined stares and holding her captive with those big hands while using those lips – those mighty, fine, full lips – to eat words of defiance right out of her mouth. Breaking down her defenses.

Okay, stop it, Gemma. What are you thinking? This is Royal for crying out loud. Stupid romance movies...

"Gem?"

"Huh?" She blinked out of her trance and her eyes brightened like he'd caught her in something.

"I asked you what you wanted to drink? Where were you just now?"

"Oh...um...I don't know. I was just thinking about something. Uh...I'll drink some—some—um—orange juice."

"No. Pick something else."

"I want some freakin' orange juice. I can have some in limited quantities."

"I'm aware of that, but the citric acid can cause heartburn, and there's no need to put yourself through that unnecessarily."

Gemma rolled her eyes. "Jeez, you're worse than Gianna."

"If by *worse* you mean *care* then you're right. What do you want to drink?"

"Nothing. Just forget it."

Royal opened the refrigerator and took out two bottles of water. When her food was warm, he brought the bowl over to her then set down chugging water while watching her eat.

"I thought you didn't like oatmeal," she said.

"I don't."

"But yet, you keep some in the house."

"No. I got up early this morning and made a trip to the grocery store specifically for oatmeal."

"Really?" she asked, her cheeks turning a shade of pink. Suddenly, she wasn't as mad about the orange juice any longer.

"Yes, really."

"Well, thank you."

"You're welcome, Gemma. Always."

Gemma opened her bottle of water and looked at him wondering why he was staring at her so intently. Why his eyes seemed darker. Maybe he wasn't in a good mood this morning she surmised and kept that to the forefront of her mind. "How did *you* sleep, Royal?"

"I didn't get much sleep."

Aha! Lack of sleep. That definitely contributed to a crabby mood, didn't it?

"Why not?"

"I had a lot on my mind."

"You must be thinking about all the work you have to do tomorrow, huh?"

"Not really. Work is work. I got that handled." He watched her stir oatmeal just as he'd watched every spoonful go into her mouth. Right now, though, she was only stirring like she was too nervous to eat another bite.

"I can't tell you what kind of mood you're in right now," she confessed.

He didn't respond – only watched her eat with his eyes fixed on her lips as she chewed. And then he glanced up at her scarf again. It was starting to bother him that she felt the need to wear them around him when she didn't have to. He accepted her for who she was. It wouldn't matter if her head was completely bald. She'd still be *his* Gemma.

Gemma glanced up at him and took a sip of water. She lowered the bottle to the table and caught another glimpse of his chest and torso. Those suits he wore hid his muscles too well. Now, she could see them as clear as day, bulging out from each and every way, especially since he didn't have on a shirt. Of particular note was a tattoo over his left pectoral that read: *be true*.

"What does that mean?" she asked staring at it. "Be true."

He gave a half smile.

Finally some emotion she thought. *Positive emotion.*

"It's old," he said. "I got this tat when I was a senior in high school."

"Why?"

"I was having a hard time. Seemed like my life was falling apart back then. Looking back, I understand now that it wasn't as bad as I made it out to be. Sometimes, it's hard to see the proverbial light at the end of the tunnel when you're knee deep in quicksand."

She nodded.

He shook his head, reminiscing about it, then continued, "I was feeling down on myself...didn't have a positive outlook on anything. Didn't know what I wanted to do with my life. Who I wanted to be. *What* I wanted to be...the counselors were telling me to do this...teachers were telling me to do that. I wasn't sure if I wanted to spend four years in college and that angered my mother. She was always on my back about following in my brothers' footsteps telling me how successful they were and I never thought I could live up to her expectations...didn't know if I needed to or if I wanted to. I was ready to throw in the towel to be honest. That's when my father had a heart-to-heart with me. Told me to be true to who I was and the direction I wanted to go in without comparing myself to other people. Said I had to find my own path and determine what I wanted to do with my life. Eventually, I decided to go to college...majored in business and trust me when I say I did not want to sign on to work for St. Claire Architects."

"Why not?"

"It's challenging working with family, although I don't think I would have it any other way now."

Gemma nodded. "Speaking of working with family, I'm going to help out Gianna around the bakery a lil' bit."

"When are you starting that?"

Gemma shrugged. "I'll probably go there with her in the morning just to observe."

"Are you sure it's what you want to do?"

"What? Working with Gianna at the bakery?"

"Yes. It doesn't come across as your thing."

"It's not, but I know Gianna needs the help and I could never, ever, e-ver repay my sister for everything she's done for me."

Royal could detect the quiver in her voice when she made the statement. The truthfulness of it. "You love your sister. I can tell."

Gemma smiled. "I do. She never gave up on me. I mean, I tease her about smothering me and stuff, but she's like a mother to me. She's the best with her quirky little self."

"She is a sweetheart...just what my brother needs. She's definitely helped him out a lot."

"How?" Gemma asked, stirring the remainder of her oatmeal.

"Ramsey is one of those hardcore, real-deal, no-nonsense businessmen. He could have a good rapport with a business for years, but the *one* time they slip, it ain't nothing for him to cut 'em loose. And he'll fire you in a heartbeat. He was firing people left and right at one point like it was a sport and he was the MVP."

She chuckled. "He was *that* bad?"

"He was until he met your sister. She helped his moods a great deal."

"That's nice. That's how you know they're good together. One balances out the other."

"Yeah," Royal said. He drank some water.

"What about you, Royal? Who balances you out?"

As if he hadn't heard her question, he stared at her for a few seconds playing with the bottle cap to his water bottle then replied, "I've been busy working. That keeps me balanced." Royal finished his water then asked her, "Would you like some more oatmeal?"

"No. This was good. Thank you for making it for me."

"You're welcome, Gemma."

Gemma took a drink of water and glanced up at him again. He was still staring. "What's on tap for today?" she asked.

"You tell me, diamond girl."

"Diamond girl—that's a new one," she said trying not to blush.

"We can do whatever, though," he told her. "We can just chill around here if you would like. I don't want to tire you out."

"I'm okay for now," she said, "Or you can do something without me, you know."

"What if I don't want to do anything without you?" he asked while shooting her a penetrating gaze, hoping she'd read the implication in his eyes. He didn't *want* to do anything without her.

"Um, well in that case—"

"I tell you what..." he cut her off. "Why don't we just hang out here, then later, we'll go to dinner before I take you back to Ramsey's place. How does that sound?"

"Sounds good to me."

"That way, you can get your nap in, right?"

She smiled. "Right."

Royal stood up and grabbed another bottle of water from the fridge, at which time Gemma found herself looking, more like gawking at his body again. *Sweet mercy*. He was nothing but pure male strength and confidence.

As if knowing she was staring at him, he turned around and stared back, opening the water bottle with his eyes fixed on her. It was around this time that she saw an old scar on his lower torso near the waistband of his sweatpants – one she'd never seen before since he was usually fully clothed around her.

"What's that?" she asked, pointing.

He followed her eyes and looked down at himself. Frowned. "What's what?" he asked. Surely she wasn't talking about his...

"That," she said pointing to his scar.

"Oh. That." He smiled. "I thought you were talking about something else."

"Oh?" She blushed. "No. I didn't mean *that*. I'm talking about the scar."

"Ah...the scar." He sat down again. "When I was twenty, I was in a car accident."

"You were?"

"Yeah. It was one of those rare times it snowed in Charlotte and the accumulation of four inches actually stuck around for a while. As you'll learn, people in Charlotte already can't drive, let alone on a slick sheet of ice. So, a car comes along speeding down Hawthorne Lane then crashed right into the back of me...hit me so hard, my car flipped over. I was gouged by some glass...lost blood..."

"Oh my God!"

He smirked. "Why do you look so scared? I'm fine now."

"I know. It's just shocking and scary to hear."

"It did rattle me, but I'm fine. And that was five years ago, so..."

"Gee, maybe I should wait to get my license."

"No, you shouldn't. Your life has been on hold long enough. You're *getting* your license, Gemma."

She cracked a smile. "You say that like your word is law."

"It is where you are concerned." He took a drink of water and shot her a pair of challenging eyes, waiting for her to defy him. That defiance never came. That pleased him. It meant she was starting to understand him. To concede to his wishes. "I'm going to take a shower, but I want to give you something to think about."

"What's that, Royal?"

He stood up and stretched his arms up in the air.

Gemma took in the flexing of his brawny muscles and the dark, thick hair under his armpits. "I want you to think about what you want to do with your life?"

Gemma shrugged. "I have no idea."

"I know you don't. That's why I want you to think about it. And be ready to tell me what you come up with later," he said, then walked out of the kitchen, leaving her there at the island.

Chapter 4

As he knew she would, Gemma fell asleep on the bed in the guest bedroom right at lunchtime. As he'd done last night, he walked there to watch her rest. Admiring her this way was becoming a habit for him and she gave him plenty of time to do so. She'd slept right up until dinner, and even then he had to wake her up to eat by stroking his fingertips along the side of her face and whispering directly into her ear.

She took a moment to fully wake herself up by washing her face and checking her phone. Then she joined him in the living room.

"Did you bring a jacket?" he asked.

"No. Are we going out?"

"Yes. The restaurant is right around the corner and I thought it would be nice to walk if you're up for it."

"Yeah. I can walk."

"Okay. It's a lil' chilly, so…" Royal took off his red and black leather Yves Saint Laurent jacket and draped it over her shoulders.

"Ooh…I feel so special," she said, drowning in his jacket that smelled just like him. *Mmm.* "Thank you, Royal."

"You're welcome."

She stepped into the flats she'd left by the front door and they started the walk to the restaurant. It couldn't have been no more than ten minutes and they were already at Summit. Royal pulled out a chair and made sure Gemma was comfortable before he sat down. He told the waitress to bring water, cranberry juice and one order of barbecue shrimp for an appetizer.

"Cranberry juice?" Gemma asked when the waitress walked away.

"In lieu of alcohol. Yes."

"You can order a drink if you want, Royal. Don't let me stop you."

"I'm good." He took a long look at Gemma. She was looking around, checking out the place since this was her first time here. He felt honored to be the one to introduce her to new things and places.

"Gemma."

She focused her attention on him. Automatically, a smile came to her face. "Yes?"

"What do you really know about me other than the fact that I'm extremely good looking and work for St. Claire Architects?" Royal asked and had the gall to flash that remarkable smile of his.

She raised a brow. "*Extremely* good looking, Royal?"

"You disagree?"

"No, but gee...I ain't calling no name, but *somebody* is full of their self."

He chuckled. "I've had enough women fall to my feet to know how you women view me."

"Yeah, like those women over there staring at you right now. I see you got your own fan club. You must be popular around here in Dilworth."

He shrugged lazily. "Honestly, the worst thing a woman can do to get my attention is stare at me. I hate it."

She didn't believe him. "You hate it?"

"Very much so."

She chuckled. "You're such a hypocrite, Royal."

"Why do you say that?"

"Because you don't like to be stared at, but I know for a fact you like to stare at people."

"No, not *people*. You."

She ducked her head back, surprised by his blunt admission. "Me?"

"Yes. You." A smile grew on his face, then he continued, "I'm a troubleshooter by occupation but sometimes, my work filters into my personal life. And since I feel *personally* responsible for not realizing you were burning up with a fever that day at Ramsey's house, I feel it's my duty to ensure your well being, especially when we're together. That's why I stare at you so often. It's my way of learning you. Of picking up on things you won't say. Like right now, I've picked up on the fact that you're still tired, even though you slept for nearly six hours. Am I right?"

"Yes. I am still a little fatigued, but I'll live."

The waitress brought over their drinks and the shrimp then took their dinner orders. Gemma ordered the crusted salmon while

Royal went for a more filling dish – the New York strip.

"Thank you, Gemma said to the waitress then opened a straw for her water.

Royal took a sip of water and tossed a shrimp into his mouth. "After three months, what do you know about me, Gemma?"

"Oh, so this is the kind of dinner we're having. A question-and-answer type thing."

"No. Just conversation and I want to know how well you know me."

Gemma cleared her throat, up for the challenge. "Well, I know you're smart. You love your family. You're loyal. You're a laid back kind of guy...you don't stress over much."

He nodded. "That's a good start, but I want you to know more about me."

"Why?"

"Because I don't want our friendship to be one of those on-the-surface type situations. Friendships don't survive where there is no deeper connection. No foundation. I want you to have a connection with me."

"I *do* have a connection wit'cho big head."

He smiled endearingly at her. He was trying to be serious, and he knew she knew that, so in true Gemma fashion, she attempted to keep the conversation light, but he persisted. "It's not as strong as it could be, Gem. I don't want you to be friends with me just because my brother is married to your sister. I want you to be friends with me because you want to be—because you value me and vice versa. Because you want to be around me and actually enjoy the time we spend together. We can't get to that level if we never break the ice."

"And I suppose being by my bedside for days, feeding me chicken noodle soup by the tablespoon and rubbing your hands across my bald head wasn't enough ice breaking."

"You were sick. I was being there for you...making myself available for you, but honestly, Gemma, I didn't know you. I came to the hospital out of guilt. I was concerned for you, yes, but I also felt guilty. A troubleshooter should always know when trouble is looming, and I failed you."

"What are you talking about? You didn't fail me, Royal."

"Well, I feel like I did." Royal took a sip of cranberry juice, shaking the ice cubes in the small glass after he did so.

"I was already sick, and you're not a doctor. Just because you're a troubleshooter doesn't mean you're a superhero who's supposed to strap on a cape and fly all around Charlotte saving people from tragedy."

He smirked while picking up another shrimp, reaching across the small, round table, holding it in front of her mouth.

"No, thank you," Gemma told him.

"C'mom. Taste it."

"Grr...I hate it when you do that."

Ignoring her growls, Royal said, "Open up."

Gemma sighed heavily then opened her mouth and leaned forward to grab the shrimp with her teeth. She chewed and said, "Mmm...that's good."

"See. You should be grateful that I make you try new things," he told her.

She took another shrimp. "So, since I don't know the *deeper* things about you, how do I find out those things?"

"Ask me questions," Royal said. "Go ahead. Anything you want to know."

"Okay. Why don't you have a girlfriend?"

He chuckled. "I open up the gate for you to ask me *anything* and you want to know about a girlfriend."

"Well, yeah. You said it yourself...you're *extremely* good looking, yet, no woman."

"I chose to be single. Next question."

She chuckled. "No, don't gloss over that one so fast. Let's get *deeper*," she teased.

Royal leaned back in his chair and stroked his mustache. "Okay. Fine. I don't have a girlfriend because the women I meet aren't...genuine. It's my belief that when you're looking for someone to share your life with, you should see that person for who they are...not what they dress themselves up to be. I could go out here and pick a woman and peg her as mine, but what would I really have if all she's concerned with are the superficial things in life?"

"I thought men liked superficial? The prettiest girl gets the best looking man and that's that."

"Gemma, just because you're addicted to romance movies doesn't make you an expert on love and relationships."

"Excuse me, but have you seen *Just*

Wright?"

"You just made me watch it two weeks ago." He chuckled.

"Okay, so you know that Common's character was feeling Queen Latifah's character, but he went for her cousin, Paula Patton. Why? Because Paula was prettier. Louder. Made up. Skinny. Fit. She had everything needed to appeal to a man's eyes. Physical attraction always comes first, at least for men."

"That's not one-hundred percent true, and before you tell me all the reasons you're right, let me say this. Last year, I went to some fancy gala that Ramsey invited me to...something related to architecture...I forget. Anyway, this woman had been eyeing me all night. She was pretty, nice body—she had the looks, but whenever she opened her mouth, a swear word came out. She was cussin' like a hardcore rapper. From what you know about me, do you think I would find that attractive in a woman?"

"Well, considering I've never heard you use a swear word, I'd say no."

He clapped. "Guess you do know a lil' something about me."

The waitress set their entrees on the table then after refilling their glasses with water, she left the table again.

"Now that you've piqued my interest, I would like to know more *deeper* things," Gemma said.

Royal was cutting his steak. "Okay."

"Tell me about your last girlfriend. How long

were you together and why did you break up?"

He chewed for a moment, then after sipping more cranberry juice, he said, "Oh, that's an easy one. My last girlfriend was beautiful. She was intelligent. She had an impressive career. She was the complete package. We were together for six months."

"Why did it end?"

He shrugged. "I wasn't feeling it anymore."

"Seriously? Sounds like to me you had the perfect woman and all of a sudden, you weren't feeling it?"

"No, I wasn't. Call me crazy, but I like a woman who has flaws. Who's complicated. I don't seek perfection. I look for strength. Integrity. Loyalty. I like a woman who keeps me on my toes. Who makes me look deep within myself to see what *I'm* really made of—not a woman who tries to impress me."

"In other words, you like a chick with issues."

"If that's the way you want to put it." He ate another chunk of his steak after dipping it in A1 sauce. "What about you, Gemma?"

She laughed. "I know you're not asking me if I've ever been in a relationship."

"I am. And how long did that relationship last?"

"Very funny, Royal."

"Do you see me laughing?"

She glanced up at him. No, he wasn't laughing. He was serious again – as serious as he was this morning. Gemma wiped her mouth and said, "I've never been in a relationship.

There's your answer."

"Never?"

"No."

"Why not?"

"Why do you think?" she asked. The answer should've been obvious. "Who would want to date a sick, bald-headed chick?"

Royal grimaced. "Don't talk about yourself like that."

"It's true. Who would want to date a sick person? Especially somebody sick with cancer? Anyway, no, I haven't been in a relationship and I don't plan on ever being in one."

"Why would you do that to yourself?"

She shrugged. "*You* did it. You're perfectly fine and you're single. At least I have a valid reason for being single."

"I never said I would write off the chance of finding love. You're telling me it's not an option for you."

Gemma massaged her temples.

"I'm frustrating you," Royal said.

"It's cool. I don't expect you to understand." Gemma glanced over at Royal's fan club of women. They were still looking over at the table, catching glimpses of him. "And it's not so much about me. I *know* me. I know who I am. I know I have nothing, absolutely nothing of value to add to a relationship, which is also why I'm not thinking about one, but I also know that if by some stroke of lightning chance I was in a relationship, he—whoever he would be—is the one who would be doing the suffering. Can you imagine being in love with someone and taking them back and forth to the doctor, not knowing what will happen to them from one day to the next? I wouldn't want to put someone through that."

Yes, I can imagine that. It's been my life for weeks now, Royal thought.

"But isn't that a true test of love?"

"Yes, but my point is, why start the test? Why get involved with someone knowing I'll eventually end up either hurting them or not living up to their expectations. Right now, I'm single. I'm not unnecessarily burdening anyone with my health issues—well, except for Gianna, and hopefully, now that she has Ramsey and the baby coming, she won't be so stressed out all the time worrying about me. She has her own life now."

"I see," Royal said, but it bothered him that she hadn't once considered he actually cared about her, and even though they weren't involved, they had grown close. And what did she mean by not wanting to put anyone through the burden of driving her back and forth to the doctor because for the last three months, that was his job and it wasn't a burden. He wanted to do it. "Earlier, I asked you to think of something you would like to do with your life."

"Right...um...I couldn't come up with anything."

Royal felt a pang at his temples. "Are you telling me you have no passion? No goals?"

"I don't."

"That's absurd." He wiped his mouth.

"No, it's not," she told him. "For the last two years of my life, I've been waiting to—to die." Her voice cracked. "What's the point of having goals when you know you're not going to live long enough to fulfill them?" She stood up and excused herself to the bathroom.

"Gemma," Royal said, turning around in his chair to call after her, but she kept on walking.

He balled a fist and whacked the table because he didn't want to upset her. All he wanted was to talk candidly, to learn more about her – the *inner* her and not only the stuff she wanted him to see or the way she presented herself like she was okay. If she wasn't really okay, he wanted to know her well enough to pick up on that. And he wanted her to have a passion. What was life without passion? Without goals and something to look forward to? Still, he hadn't intended on upsetting her in the process.

"Sorry about that," she said, sitting down again after what turned out to be a brief visit to the bathroom.

He was surprised she was back so quickly, and she looked okay from what he could tell. But Gemma, he knew, had the habit of hiding her feelings. "Are you okay?" he asked. He couldn't see any evidence that she'd been crying. Maybe she just needed to take a break and reset.

"Yeah. I'm fine."

"Are you sure, Gemma?"

She worked up a smile. "I'm sure."

Royal turned his arm to glance at his watch.

"Let me get the check so we can head back."

"Okay."

* * *

At 6:30, it was already dark out. But in a bustling neighborhood like Dilworth where there were plenty of restaurants and bars, the nightlife was electrifying. Sidewalks were filled with people going this way and that way – seemed everybody had their favorite spot. So, they were in good company as they strolled down the well-lit sidewalk back to Royal's condo.

Royal turned to his right to look at Gemma. She'd been quiet since leaving the restaurant and he knew it had something to do with his line of questioning. "Are you okay?"

"Yeah. I'm okay." She glanced up at a couple of women in workout gear running toward and on past them. "Royal, why do you want me to have a passion?"

"Everybody needs a passion in life. It'll motivate you...keep you going. It sounds weird, I know, but solving problems for a living is mine."

She glanced over and up at him, taking in the silhouette of his face. "At least you know that. What I was trying to tell you in the restaurant was, I never took the time to have a passion because I truly didn't think I would live long enough to ever be anything. My doctor told me I had two months to live."

Royal grasped her left hand into his right.

"Yet, you're still here."

Their eyes met, smiles grew when they looked at each other. They took a few more steps and Royal became hyper-aware of her hand in his grasp. It felt good holding her hand especially since he'd already considered her his. And she wasn't the least bit nervous. She was just being herself. They were being *them*.

"When we were talking about relationships earlier, you said you had nothing of value to offer anyone," Royal said.

"I—"

"Wait, wait, wait—let me finish," he told her, applying gentle pressure to her hand.

"Okay. Proceed."

"You have value and plenty of it. You fought cancer and won. Do you know how valuable you are to people who are going through the very thing you went through? You have a message of hope. You are a walking billboard of hope for a lot of people, Gemma, and not just in instances of people going through cancer, but any kind of trial life throws at them, you know."

Gemma nodded. "You're right. I never looked at it that way."

"You really need to. And stop being so hard on yourself. You are an amazing woman."

Amazing. She grinned a little.

"What are you laughing at?"

"You. You sound like an old man giving me pieces of wisdom and you're only twenty-five."

He lazily kicked a pebble along their path and said, "Funny you should say that. Mother says I'm young in the face but she swears I have an old soul."

"She's right, although I will say it's the beard that makes you look older." *And ruggedly handsome.*

"I've heard that a time or two."

"So, is your mother right? Do you feel like an old soul?"

"Sometimes."

They turned the block and were now on his street.

"While you were napping today, I was brainstorming...trying to determine what kinds of activities you might find interesting and I came up with something."

"Which is...?"

"Becoming a volunteer at the children's cancer center here...offering hope and support to young victims of cancer."

"Wow. Volunteering...that's actually a really good idea."

"And while you're doing that, you can also find our first patient for The Gemma Jacobsen Foundation once we get that off the ground."

Gemma glanced over at him and said, "Stop."

He smiled. "What?"

"You're going to make me cry."

"Don't do that," he told her as they headed up the stairs. He wasn't left-handed by any means, but he wasn't about to let her hand go to unlock the door, so he used his left hand instead, holding her hand still as they walked inside. "Did you pack your bag already?"

"For the most part. I only have a few more items to put in it."

"Okay," he said. He wasn't ready for her to leave, but he knew he had to take her back home.

"Hey, do you want to let my hand go so I can do that?" she asked, amused.

"You could just stay with me one more night."

"Oh, please. I know you've had enough of me. And, you have to work in the morning and I need to go check on Gianna."

"Why do you need to check on Gianna? Ramsey got that locked down."

"Exactly. That's why I need to check on her." Gemma grinned. "I'm kidding. I trust Ramsey with my sister. I just miss her and *don't* tell her I said that."

Royal smiled. "I won't." He released her hand finally.

"Okay. Let me get my stuff. I'll be ready in about ten minutes."

Royal stood there watching her walk down the hall and toward the guest bedroom, thinking of how quickly their time together passed. He didn't want her to go, but what choice did he have?

Chapter 5

On the drive to Lake Norman, Gemma reclined her seat and pretended to be sleeping, but all she could think about was Royal. He said it in a joking way, but somehow she knew he didn't want her to leave. He would've been perfectly okay with her staying for another day. Week. Maybe even a month. But why? And why did he want to know her deeper? To know the inner workings of her? To go below the surface, he'd said. Could it actually be that he was interested?

With her eyes still closed, she smiled. *Nah. No way. There's no way a man as fine, sexy and charming as him could be remotely interested in me. He's just being nice to me because he feels sorry for me...sorry that my life has been so drab for so long. That I had cancer. That he didn't put his troubleshooting skills to work to diagnose my temperature spike. Still, that doesn't equal interest...*

Or, it could have just been the way he was – friendly. He knew they would see each other regularly since she lived with Gianna and Ramsey. Why not develop a friendship? Why not get to know her? Then again, Regal and

Romulus weren't trying to know every aspect of her life. They seemed to be okay with the occasional small talk. Royal, however, was completely different. He wanted to *know* her. Talk to her. Be with her.

Royal glanced over at Gemma. Was that a smile on her face, and if so, had she gone to sleep that fast? Was she dreaming? If so, what was she dreaming about? Dang, he had it bad – wanted to know everything about her. In his twenty-five years of life, he couldn't recall ever wanting to know everything about a woman. Even his last girlfriend – the woman who had the whole package as he described – wasn't enough to keep him. He'd broken it off with her because it wasn't what he wanted. And he'd done the same with the two, semi-long term relationships he had before whole-package-girl – broke it off.

He had specific tastes when it came to women, and in his mind, he imagined every man did. But his went like this – she had to be beautiful – not society's standard of beauty, but beautiful in her own way with her own unique characteristics. There was nothing like staring into the face of a beautiful woman he loved. And his ideal woman had to have drive. Ambition. He didn't want a lazy, unmotivated woman. He wanted someone with the same work ethic as him. Additionally, she had to be sweet – a genuinely good person at heart. He could thank his mother for instilling that attribute in him. Bernadette St. Claire was the sweetest woman he knew. All of his brothers loved and had a healthy respect for their mother, but being the youngest, he was the closest to her – the last one to leave home. He truly appreciated all the talks she'd had with him about life. It made him realize what he wanted out of life, especially when it came to love.

He looked at Gemma again. She was skinny in his opinion although she still had a tight little body and a plump apple bottom. She wore size eight clothes, and the woman didn't have enough energy to do much of anything. He knew it was her body's way of making her slow down as she was still recovering from the surgery, but he somehow wished he could help speed up the recovery process.

One step at a time, Royal.

He had to remind himself of that because the truth of the matter was, Gemma almost didn't make it. Before he came into her life, Ramsey was already with Gianna and aware of Gemma's diagnosis. If Ramsey hadn't stepped in and used his money, power and influence to get Gemma to the right doctors, she probably wouldn't be here today. He would be forever grateful to his brother for the care and concern he showed to her.

When he pulled up in Ramsey's driveway, he palmed Gemma's thigh and squeezed it. "Gemma, we're here."

She opened her eyes and stretched until her hands touched the roof of the car. "That was quick." Still reclined, she yawned and said, "Do I have to get out?"

"Yes. You'll get a cramp in your neck if you stay in that position."

"Alright, alright." She clicked off her seatbelt, then pressed the seat adjustment button to raise the seat to an upright position. After stretching again, she opened the door and got out. Stretched her body some more.

"Am I going to have to carry you to the house?" Royal asked.

"No."

"Stretch one more time and I'm throwing you over my shoulder."

"You ain't gon' do nothing."

He cracked a corner smile. "Try me. You're already as light as a feather. It wouldn't take nothing for me to scoop your lil' butt up."

Gemma faked a yawn and extended her hands in the air like she was actually stretching.

"Okay, that's it," Royal said.

Before he could get to her, she took off jogging for the front stairs. He was right on her heels with her bag.

"You better run."

She was giggling as she ran up the stairs, to the opened door where she saw her straight-faced sister. "Gianna!" Gemma said excited, embracing Gianna.

"Don't *Gianna* me," Gianna said hugging her back and at the same time, watching as Royal ascended the stairs. She glared at him.

He smiled. It took a special kind of person to hug someone and mean-mug someone else at precisely the same time.

When she released Gemma, Gianna asked, "Royal, what have you been doing to my sister?"

Royal chuckled. "Doing *to* your sister?"

"Yeah." Gianna crossed her arms. "What have you been doing to my sister?"

"Nothing much. I've been taking good care of her. Right, Gem?"

"Yep," Gemma said.

Gianna glared more as Royal approached her.

"And how are you, Gianna?" he asked, hugging her even though her arms were still folded over her chest.

Gemma had since gone inside of the house.

"I'm fine now that I know my sister is okay."

Royal released her. "I know how to take care of Gemma. You have absolutely nothing to worry about when she's with me."

"Okay, but the next time you want to *take* her, can you run it by me first?"

"Yes, ma'am," Royal said with a smirk on his face.

Ramsey stepped out onto the porch and wrapped his arms around Gianna from behind and said close to her ear, "Baby, why don't you go ahead and go back inside. It's a little chilly out here. I don't want you to get sick."

"Okay," she said.

"Ay, I'm not going to stay long," Royal told them. "Let me put Gem's bag in the foyer."

He stepped inside right behind Gianna placing Gemma's bag on the floor.

Gianna continued on toward the kitchen,

leaving the two men in the foyer.

"How was it?" Ramsey asked Royal.

"How was what?"

"Having a woman over at the bachelor palace?"

Royal chuckled. "I've had women at my place before, Ram. Plenty of 'em."

"I'm sure you have, but by your own admission, there's something *different* about this particular woman."

Royal cracked a smile, one he couldn't much help. "I'll talk to you about that tomorrow. Let me say goodnight to Gemma and get going or you won't see me tomorrow. It's already late."

Royal jogged upstairs and walked down the hallway toward Gemma's room. When he arrived, he found the door open with her sitting on the bed, taking off her shoes. He leaned his six-feet-four-inch, muscular body against the doorframe and crossed his arms, watching her. "Do you need some help with that?" he asked.

She looked up. Smiled. "I think I can manage." She removed her other shoe and rubbed her toes.

"I'm getting ready to head back home," he told her. "Come give your boy some love?"

She giggled. "*Give your boy some love*," she repeated, standing up. She walked right up to him and wrapped her arms tight around him. "You're a trip. You know that?"

"You're one to talk," he said, embracing her gentle enough to be gentlemanlike but firm enough to leave an impression. "If you need anything, call me."

"Sure, Royal," she said as he loosened his hold from around her. Looking up into his eyes, she playfully said, "If I break a nail, I'll be sure to call you."

"Why do you think everything is a joke, girl?" he asked, wanting to snatch her up into his arms and hold her there while losing his tongue somewhere in her mouth. He was tempted. Truth be told, he'd *been* tempted for a long time now, but as he always did, he got ahold of himself and kept his composure. Lately, he found himself struggling with self-control in that regard.

"Loosen up," she said, balling fists and pushing against his chest. "I'm just kidding."

"Well, I'm serious this time, Gemma. If you need me for anything, call. Alright?" he asked, nudging her chin up so she looked at him.

"Okay. I will."

He embraced her again. Tighter this time. "Goodnight, Gemma."

"Goodnight, Royal."

Reluctantly releasing her, he turned and walked away, headed back downstairs and spoke briefly to Ramsey before he left.

Chapter 6

"How was your weekend with lover boy?" Gianna asked stepping into Gemma's room as if she'd been down the hallway lurking, waiting for the exact moment Royal left.

"Look at this...I have a revolving door tonight," Gemma quipped.

Gianna walked in and sat on the bed next to Gemma. "How do you feel?"

"I'm fine, Gianna. Royal took good care of me."

"I bet he did," she snarled, narrow-eyed.

Gemma grinned at the implication of her tone. "I don't know why you lookin' all crazy. Royal *did* take good care of me. He's harmless."

"I didn't know you were going to stay with him for the weekend."

"Then that makes two of us. It was his idea. He said it would give you and Ramsey some privacy. I agreed." She shrugged. "Besides, I didn't think it was a big deal."

Gianna's brows raised. "Anytime you're not with me, is a big deal. I need to make sure you take your medication."

"Correction—*I* need to make sure I take my medication, Gianna. Look, you're going to have a son or daughter of your own in like what? Six...seven months? I can't have you stressing about me when you have a baby on the way."

"I'm not stressed. I just need to know that you're okay at all times. It would've been nice to have a heads up that you were going to be staying with Royal."

"Okaaay," Gemma conceded. "I'll remember that for next time."

Gianna frowned. "Next time? You're already planning on staying with him again?"

"No, Gianna. This was just a one-time deal. And it was for you and Ramsey."

Gianna turned up her lips.

Gemma shook her head. "Jeez, okay, I don't know what it is you're thinking, but in case this is it, let me clarify. Royal St. Claire is not interested in me." She untied her scarf, placed it on the bed and massaged her short hair. She felt comfortable with Gianna seeing it – no one else.

"Could've fooled me."

"What does that mean?" Gemma asked.

"It means, Royal has a thing for you and you can't even see it."

Gemma cackled. "Royal does not have a *thing* for me."

"Oh, yes he does. Now that I have experience with a man, I can read the signs."

"Oh, goodness. Here we go..."

"I'm surprised you don't see them. You have to have picked up on it by now."

Gemma turned red in the face as she laughed. "There's nothing to pick up on,

67

Gianna. I promise you there isn't."

"You've never seen Royal staring at you? He stares at you a lot, just like Ramsey does to me."

"That's only because he has this obsession with making sure people are okay. It's his job. He's a...um...whatchamacallit...a troubleshooter."

Gianna grinned. "Girl, do you even know what a troubleshooter is?"

"Yeah. A person who shoots trouble. Duh." Gemma grinned.

"Come on, Gemma. Be serious."

"It's hard to be serious when you're trying to imply that Royal has a thing for me. It's not possible. I'm not even his type."

"Doesn't matter. I wasn't Ramsey's type. Now, we're married with a baby on the way. I'm telling you—there's something more."

"Gianna, you didn't even know Ramsey was feeling you until I told you so."

"Then I'm returning the favor, baby sis. Maybe you're so close to Royal, you can't see it, but I've been watching him—like the way you two were dancing on the yacht Saturday afternoon. He had you pulled so close to him, I'm surprised *you're* not the one with the baby on the way."

Gemma couldn't help but laugh. "Excuse me but when did you find the time to watch us dance? I thought Ramsey had you occupied."

"I wasn't so occupied that I couldn't see the way Royal was looking at you."

Gemma brushed off her words. She didn't

want to admit it but she had caught Royal staring at her on several occasions. And then there was the way he looked at her – a way in which she couldn't describe – not to mention the way he seemed to enjoy hugging her. Touching her. "Enough about your theories. Can we change the subject?"

"To what?"

"I dunno...let's say, you. Do you have morning sickness?"

"No."

"You haven't been sick at all?"

Gianna beamed. "No. Not at all. That why Ramsey's mother seems to think I'm having a boy. She said she didn't get sick with any of her boys when she was carrying."

"Well, that's great you're feeling okay. I know Ramsey is through the roof excited."

"He is."

Gemma stretched. "Well, I hate to rush you out of here, but I need to take a shower and go to bed."

"What's the matter? Didn't get much sleep at Royal's?"

"I got plenty of sleep. But today, we took a walk to a restaurant near his condo and walked back. I dozed off in the car on the way here and now I'm ready to pass out."

"Okay, then," Gianna said standing.

"Oh, and I'm going with you to the bakery tomorrow, so don't leave me."

"Why don't you wait until Tuesday, Gem? I don't want to tire you out."

"I'll be fine. I want to go ahead and get

started. Royal thinks it's important for me to do something."

"Does he?"

"Yes. He wants me to have something special that I like to do. He thinks I could volunteer at the children's cancer hospital— says I could offer hope to the kids."

Gianna smiled. "That's actually not a bad idea."

"I know."

"And Royal came up with this on his own?"

"He did."

"That proves right there that he's been thinking about you."

"Maybe, but not in the way you're suggesting. It's certainly not the way Ramsey sits around and thinks about you."

Gianna looked delightfully happy. "Wow. It's so different watching you in the very same position I was in and not being able to see what's going on right in front of your eyes."

"The only thing I want to see in front of my eyes are my eyelids. Now, skedaddle on up out of my room. You know Ramsey gon' call a search party if you stay too long."

"Whatever." Gianna laughed. "Goodnight, Gem."

"Goodnight. I love you." She looked at Gianna's stomach and said, "I mean, *y'all.*"

"*We* love you, too." Gianna walked to the door.

Gemma waited until Gianna exited, then removed the rest of her clothes. She stepped in the shower, seriously considering the things

Gianna was saying. What if...

What if Royal really liked her beyond a simple friendship? She grinned. Not likely. Royal wasn't just any random man she'd met. He was a St. Claire for goodness sakes. At twenty-five, he had his stuff together. He wasn't confused about life. He seemed to have carved a clear path for himself. Surely, she was a diversion from that path, but that's it. A diversion – not a fixture. There was no way he was the least bit interested in her besides the fact that he wanted to help her.

Royal the *troubleshooter* wanted to make her life easier using his professional prowess in doing so. She didn't see anything wrong with that, besides the fact that he could be a little pushy and insistent. And it didn't help that he was drop-dead gorgeous. She had to will herself to fight an attraction to him, but she'd done it. She had developed a plan to combat fantasizing about him. Whenever she found herself lost in his eyes, she'd picture in her mind what the *Royal* woman would look like – like a freakin' supermodel – not a cancer survivor with hardly any hair, no body and no...nothing. So brushing off everything Gianna had said, she persisted and maintained that she and Royal were just friends and nothing more. That's the way it was. The way it would always be.

Chapter 7

"What's up with you, Royal?" Ramsey asked, stepping inside of Royal's office after their Monday morning status meeting. "You almost lost it in there for absolutely nothing."

"Because you don't listen, Ram. I told you, Regal and Romulus, three weeks ago, that we needed to find a new vendor for the Paris project. None of you listened. But since Basile has brought it to your attention, now, all of a sudden, it's a hot-button issue. How about listening to your brother over some fancy talking French dude? Dang."

"You're right, Royal. You're right. My bad. I was going through some things with Gianna when you tried to tell me about the vendor issue and I should've been more focused on work."

"No. You should've been focused on Gianna. I just—" Royal sighed and dropped his head. Frustrated.

"What is it, Royal?"

"It's Gemma."

Concern quickly came to Ramsey's face. If something was wrong with Gemma, it would, in turn, affect Gianna and he couldn't have that. "What's wrong with Gemma?"

"Okay, let me be more specific. There's nothing wrong with her. This is about me and my feelings for her."

"Oh, I see," Ramsey said, picking up on the problem right away. He already knew his brother had feelings for Gemma. "What seems to be the issue?"

Royal looked up toward the ceiling and blew out a breath. "The issue is, when I'm here—whenever I'm away from her, I can't stop thinking about her. Right now while I'm sitting here talking to you, she's on my mind."

"Why do you think that is?"

"Because I've developed these *feelings* for her that won't go away."

"*Won't go away* implies that you've tried to shake it."

"I have, for *her* sake. Man, Gemma has no idea how I feel about her. She sees me the same way she sees you—like a big brother."

"And how do you see her?"

Royal thought for a moment, but it didn't take long to reply, "I see her as a woman I could share my life with."

"Whoa," Ramsey said. He took a seat in one of the leather chairs in Royal's office and said, "Okay, let's not get crazy."

"I'm not crazy. That's how I feel about her."

"How is that possible, Royal, when you've only known her for three months?"

"You knew Gianna for less time when you two got married."

"That was different. It was a Wedded Bliss

situation, well, partly. Whatever the case, this isn't your method of operation."

Royal sat back and crossed his arms over his chest. "Okay, so you tell me how I operate since you know me better than I know myself."

"You're trying to be sarcastic, but I do know how you operate, Royal. First of all, you get bored with women easily. The last woman you dated owned a business. She was a looker, too, and you dropped her just like that," Ramsey said and snapped his finger for added emphasis.

"I wasn't feeling her. What am I supposed to do? Force myself into a relationship with someone just because they're a catch? And to clarify, just because the woman was a catch doesn't mean she was *my* catch."

"And Gemma is?"

"I have a connection with Gemma."

"You have a connection with Gemma, yet, she has no idea how you feel about her. She hasn't picked up on any vibes. Wouldn't you think if you were feeling a woman, she would have a hint you were into her?"

"Not Gemma. She's never been in a relationship before. She's young and—"

"And she's not for you," Ramsey said.

Royal frowned. "You can't tell me who I can and can't date."

"Royal, I'm telling you for your own good. Keep this thing with Gemma on a friendship level."

"I can't."

"Why not?"

"Because I love her."

"You...you what?"

"I. Love. Her," Royal said intentionally slow hoping Ramsey would get it this time.

Ramsey took a minute to let it sink in then shook his head. "Sorry, but I can't let you hurt her. History shows you'll drop her just like all the rest."

"I won't. She's different."

"Why? Because of the cancer?"

"No. Because she's strong and there's an ambitious woman inside of her. I want to bring her out. I mean she's already smart. She's funny. She has *the* most beautiful smile I've ever seen in my life. I love her, Ramsey."

Ramsey frowned.

"What do you have against me and her?" Royal asked.

"I don't like the idea of you dating her and dropping her when you're done. That's all I can see in my head. I don't want you to hurt Gemma. Hurting her would be hurting Gianna. She doesn't need to be stressed out because she's troubled about what you may or may not do to her sister."

"Then I give you my word. I won't hurt her. I really do love her, Ramsey."

Ramsey raised a brow. "And you're sure about that after three months?"

"Positive."

Ramsey sighed deeply and rubbed his mustache. Thinking. "You haven't told her how you feel?"

"No."

"Then let me give you a word of advice—be a friend first. Don't move so quickly. I think that was your problem in your last relationship. You were so in a hurry to be in a relationship, you didn't take the time to really know the woman. Get to know Gemma."

"I do know her."

"Then take the time to know her better. What harm could come from taking things slow? And she's still in the recuperating stage of her recovery, man. Let the friendship build organically. Don't rush it. If it's meant to be, everything else will fall into place."

"Alright. I'll try to take your advice," Royal said, swiveling in his black executive chair.

"Good."

Ramsey stared at his brother for a moment and then asked, "What is it about her?"

Royal smiled. "I just told you. I think mostly, though, it's just—just her. I like how comfortable she is around me."

"You know that'll change the minute she knows you're feeling her."

"Yeah. Another reason I should take it slow, I guess," Royal said, tapping a pen on the desktop.

"Yep." Ramsey stood up. "You know she's at the bakery with Gianna today, right?"

"Oh, so she *did* go? She was so tired last night, I didn't think she would wake up in time."

"Yeah, she went. I'm going by there at lunch if you want to tag along and see your girl," Ramsey said.

"Cool. Ay, let me know when you're leaving."

"Yep," Ramsey said, exiting the office.

Chapter 8

Gemma had been working nonstop since arriving at the bakery with Gianna. She got a lesson on how to make vanilla cupcakes and now she was placing a new, freshly frosted batch in the display counter at the front when she saw Ramsey and Royal walk in.

"Um, why are y'all coming up in here looking like a couple of Federal agents?" Gemma asked.

Ramsey smirked. "I'm here for my set of sweet lips. Where is she?"

Gemma shrugged. "She's probably back there somewhere hiding from you. You know how she do."

"Yes, all too well," Ramsey said, stepping behind the counter. He gave Gemma a kiss on the temple and asked, "How are you, peanut?"

"I'm good. Gianna's keeping me busy."

"I'm sure she is. This place does get pretty crowded, but," Ramsey glanced at his Rolex. "It's almost one. The rush is almost over."

"Good," Gemma said. "Maybe now I can get a chance to sit down."

While Ramsey continued on to the back, Gemma turned to look at Royal. "So, Ramsey's here to stalk my sister, obviously. What brings you by, *prince* Royal? Here to check out the booming cupcake scene at the University City Boardwalk?"

He grinned. "Nah. Gianna's cupcakes are delicious, but I, for one, like to keep my abs nice and tight."

And they're certainly tight and nice for that matter. Gemma still couldn't get the image of his bare chest and torso out of her head, not that she wanted to. She gave him a full once over, looking at his expensive leather shoes and a gray suit that looked like he just wore it straight out of Neiman Marcus. No wrinkles. Just perfect creases on a most perfect body. "Okay, so what's up? You and Ramsey riding around troubleshooting, *causing* trouble or what?"

"No. I rode with him over here because I knew you were here."

She lifted a brow. "You came to see me?"

"Yes, Gemma," he said, giving her a pointed stare. "I came to see you."

Ugh. Sure you did...

She hated how sinfully handsome men toyed with women's emotions just because they could. He came to see her.

Yeah...

Right...

He could've come up with something better than that, like maybe he and Ramsey had to run out to a job site and Ramsey wanted to stop by the bakery to see Gianna before returning to the office. That sounded more plausible.

She glanced up at him. He was still staring.

She wondered why, but caught up in the magnificence of his attractiveness, she remained without a voice.

"Can you take a break for a minute?" he asked.

She frowned, darted her head back and glanced around before looking at him again. "Who? Me?" she asked, placing a hand on her chest.

He chuckled. "Yes. You. Why are you getting brand new on a brother all of a sudden?"

"I just...I...um...I'm fine. I'm not getting *brand new*...whatever that means to you. I just...um—" Gemma swallowed the thick lump that threatened her voice. *What are you doing, Gemma? All that crap Gianna told you about Royal last night is messing with your head and has you acting strange. And not just any kind of strange, but Gianna strange. Oh no. I'm becoming my sister. Crap. Crap. Crap!*

"Gemma."

Gemma closed her eyes the moment she heard him call her name. Instead of trying to shake off the nerves that had her *becoming her sister* and making an attempt to save face, the strangeness continued when she opened her left eye and kept the right one closed.

Royal chuckled. "Something wrong with your eye?"

"Nope. Something wrong wit'cho face?" she shot back.

Royal frowned, stroking his hand down his beard. "You're acting weird," he said. "Are you okay?"

"Y-ye-yeah. I'm fine." She closed both eyes and did a reset, opening them both at the same time now.

"You're back."

"Ta-da!" she said, silently chastising herself for acting like a flake. *Get it together, Gemma. Jeez.*

"Can you take a walk with me?" he asked, undeterred by her antics.

"Um..."

"If you can't—"

"Wait...let me check with Gianna first," Gemma said. "Be right back." Gemma walked to the back to find Gianna sitting on the desk in her office with Ramsey standing in front of her. All she could hear was kissing, moaning and lip-smacking noises.

"Ew. Don't y'all get enough of each other at home?" Gemma asked.

Ramsey grinned. "I can never get enough of my sweet cupcake."

"O-kay. Gianna, if you can hear me, I'm going to take a walk with the prince real quick. I'll be back shortly."

"Take your time," Ramsey said. "I'll fill in while you're gone. No need to rush."

"Okay. Thanks, and remember – the baby needs air, Ramsey. Gianna can't breathe with your tongue blocking her windpipe."

Ramsey chuckled while Gianna looked embarrassed. "I'll keep that in mind."

Gemma took off her apron and headed to the front of the bakery where Royal was waiting for her. "Ready?" she asked him.

"Yeah," Royal said as they headed to the door together. He pushed it open and held it for her to exit ahead of him.

"Thanks."

"You're welcome."

Following his lead, they took a few steps in the direction of the wooden bridge in front of Boardwalk Billy's.

"You're looking mighty dapper in that suit, by the way," she told him.

"You act like this is the first time you've seen me in a suit."

"It's the first time I've seen you in *this* one. You usually don't wear gray, but it suits you. No pun intended."

He grinned again. "Well, thank you."

"You're welcome." Silence passed between them before Gemma asked, "So, where are we walking to?"

"Nowhere," he said, stopping at the highest point of the bridge. He leaned against the railings and stared out into the water. A few people were in pedal boats, he noticed, while some people sat on benches, throwing bread crumbs to the ducks and geese.

Gemma leaned against it, too, taking in the scenery. It was a mostly cloudy day, but whenever the sun peeked from behind the clouds, the reflection on the water was bright enough to make her squint. "It's a beautiful day, isn't it?"

"It is. I love this time of year."

"Me, too." Gemma looked out into the water again. "Hey, I was thinking about the things you said yesterday."

"About what?"

"You know...about me having something I like to do."

He nodded. "Okay."

"I was wondering—why do you care whether or not I'm passionate about something?"

"I think it'll help you...give you something to work for. Something to live for. Something to look forward to when you wake up in the mornings."

"I suppose..."

"Did you have lunch?" he inquired.

"I did."

"What'd you eat?"

"Gianna went to Panera and got some broccoli cheddar soup."

"Oh."

"I can't wait until I get my driver's license so I can go get my own soup."

"Have you been studying the driver's handbook?"

"No. I'm kinda freaked out about it."

He turned to look at her. "About the test or driving?"

"Both."

"There's nothing to it, really."

"It is when you've never been behind the wheel of a car at twenty years of age. Gosh. I sound so pathetic."

Royal grimaced. He hated to hear her talk about herself in such a negative light. "It's cool, Gem. One step at a time. You gotta crawl before you can walk."

"Well, if I don't get my license, I'll be doing a little of both."

He chuckled.

So did she.

"How has it been helping Gianna at the bakery today?" he asked shifting his body to look directly at her.

"It's cool. I just found myself nodding off a few times."

"That's not good."

"I know. I need to talk to the doctor about this fatigue."

"You know what the doctor is going to say, right?"

"No."

"That you need to exercise. Tiredness doesn't go away from sleeping. Being active is more effective."

"Well, I doubt very seriously that my doctor is going to tell me to get a gym membership to Planet Fitness."

"You're right, but nice walks wouldn't hurt. You gotta get off that rump and move around, girl."

Royal withheld a smile, but when he felt Gemma staring at him, he looked at her and couldn't help but laugh.

Her eyes narrowed. "You're not funny. You know that, right?"

"Whatever you say, Gem. When is your next appointment?"

"Thursday."

"What time?" he asked, intentionally sliding his hands across the railing until one of them touched hers.

She shrugged. "I think it's nine-something."

"Can you give me the exact time beforehand, please?"

"Why, Royal? You don't have to take me this time. Gianna's—"

"Gianna's not taking you, so forget about it. I am."

A breeze chilled her face as she looked at him, but something in the pit of his eyes made her feel warm all over.

"Okay. If that's what you want," she told him.

His gaze settled on her lips. "Yes. It's exactly what I want, Gemma."

She turned away from him and looked back out at the water. *Why is he staring at my lips?* It was on the top of her tongue to ask, but thinking it through, she decided against doing so.

"Are you working at the bakery tomorrow?"

"No. I had planned on calling the children's hospital and inquiring about volunteering."

Royal smiled, glad to hear she was giving his suggestion serious consideration. "Before you jump all the way in, make sure it's something you really want to do, Gemma."

"It is. Well, it's a start I should say. Who knows? It may lead me down another path toward my *true* calling since it's your belief that I actually have one."

"Everyone does." Royal stood straight up taking his hands off of the railing. "Anyway, I imagine Ramsey has gotten his afternoon

Gianna fix, so let's head back."

Gemma chuckled. "Okay."

He was walking slow, almost like he didn't want to go back and she fell into stride beside him, taking in the scent of his glorious cologne that played with her sanity when the wind caught it just right.

"Are you staying with Gianna until closing?"

"She's the one with the driver's license, so yeah."

"If you get tired and want to leave before then, let me know. I'll come pick you up."

Like I'm really going to call you to come pick me up and take me all the way to Lake Norman only so you'll have to turn around and drive all the way back to Dilworth. No thanks. "I'll be fine, Royal."

"Just acknowledge you heard my offer."

"Yes. I heard your offer, your highness, and I appreciate it."

Royal opened the door to the bakery and allowed her to enter. Ramsey and Gianna were kissing by the register.

"Ahem," Gemma said.

"We've been busted again," Ramsey said against Gianna's lips.

Gianna smiled, then looked at Gemma. "Sorry, sis. I couldn't help myself."

Gemma rolled her eyes.

"Take it easy for the rest of the day, sweetness," Ramsey said to Gianna. "I'll see you tonight."

"Okay," Gianna said. "Love you."

"I love you, too, sweetness."

Royal looked at Gemma, wanting so badly to echo the words that Ramsey had spoken to Gianna – only his would be directed to Gemma. Instead, he settled for, "See you later, Gem."

"See ya," Gemma replied.

Chapter 9

Later that evening after helping Gianna close up the bakery, the women were on the way home when Gemma asked, "What does it feel like to be in love?"

"Um...gee, I guess that answer would be different depending on whoever you ask."

"Well, I'm asking you, Gianna. I've watched you fall in love with Ramsey right before my eyes, and y'all can't keep your hands off of each other. So, tell me. How is it?"

"It's an amazing feeling that has me floating sometimes, which is crazy because it's something I thought I didn't want. Actually, I didn't think I could handle it, you know, but Ramsey's the best."

"Royal said he's mean. At work, that is..."

Gianna laughed. "He's not *mean*. He's a perfectionist when it comes to his job and if he feels like somebody isn't doing what they're supposed to be doing, he doesn't have a problem calling them out on it. And Royal can't talk much about Ramsey when he's basically the same way. That's why they don't get along all that well."

"Really, because when I see them together,

they're laughing it up—having a jolly ol' St. Claire time," Gemma said.

"Right. When they're around each other *outside* of work, their cool. At work, it's another story. It's the strangest thing."

Gemma took a mental note then stared out the window. "Royal is very particular. He has a certain way he likes things to go. I wonder if he's even aware of how demanding he is, or if he thinks it's normal to have such high expectations of people."

"Of *people*, or you?"

"Well, I'll use myself as an example." She shifted her position in the seat so she was looking at Gianna. Then she continued. "He talks to me like I'm his daughter or something. And he has these goals in his head for me, like this volunteering thing for instance."

"I thought you liked that idea?"

"I do, but it's...I don't know. I'm probably just trippin'." She glanced out the window again and said, "No. I'm not trippin'. He is demanding. For example, I told him you were taking me to the doctor on Thursday and he said, *no, I'm taking you to the doctor.*"

"And what did you say after he said that?"

"I just...I don't...I don't even remember because *whatever* I said, if it was the opposite of what he wanted to do, he'd shoot my idea down. He acts like he's *soo* much older than I am. There's only a five-year difference between us and yet it seems like we're at least a decade apart. Anyway, I'm rambling. Just, FYI, Royal volunteered himself to take me to the doctor—

again—on Thursday, so I guess you don't have to do it."

Gianna glanced at her sister then returned her attention back to driving when she said, "You know you don't have to give in to him every time."

"Yeah, I know."

"Then why do you?"

She smirked. "That's a good question."

"I know why," Gianna said.

"Why?"

"Because you like him."

Gemma chewed on her lip. "A little bit, yes," she admitted.

"No, not a little bit...more like a lotta bit."

Gemma laughed.

"Laugh all you want, but you two have been spending a lot of time together. That's how it all starts off in the beginning. Trust me. I know."

"Yeah, but it wasn't supposed to be like this. It's like, since I was in the hospital, he formed an attachment to me and our friendship grew legs and took off. I don't think neither of us expected to be besties after I was discharged from the hospital."

"Okay, so what do you do about it now?"

She shrugged. "Don't know. I'm still in friend mode and that's where I intend on staying."

"So, you have no feelings for him at all?"

"What kind of feelings?" Gemma asked.

"Come on, Gem. You know exactly what I mean."

"No, elaborate."

"Alright...like do you feel all tingly around him and stuff?"

Gemma laughed. "Tingly? That's the best you can come up with? Tingly?"

"Okay, do you feel vibes when you're with him?" Gianna asked as she pulled up in the driveway, noticing Ramsey standing on the front porch like he'd been waiting on her.

"I see your man lurking," Gemma said.

Gianna chuckled. "Don't try to change the subject. Do you feel vibes when you're with Royal?"

"Vibes?" Gemma asked, playing dumb.

"Yeah. Like a flutter of butterflies in your stomach."

"Yes, but that's only because Royal's so freakin' good looking. And because he stares at me...finds excuses to touch me."

Gianna lifted a brow. "Touch you?"

"Yeah, and I'm not talking about grabbing my booty or anything like that—"

"He sure was grabbing your booty when we were on the yacht."

Gemma giggled. "But he was just playing around. He wasn't being serious. I'm talking about touching me in subtle ways. And sometimes, he'd just hold my hand when we're together like we're a couple. Remember when I told you we went out to dinner Sunday evening?"

"Yeah."

"When we were walking back to his place, he held my hand, almost as if I was his girlfriend.

Like he didn't care if someone saw him holding my hand...didn't care if he gave the impression that I was his girl, and the whole time we're walking, I'm trying not to read too much into it, but I start to ask myself why he would do that? Why reach for my hand?"

"Holding hands could be considered a friendly gesture."

"On what planet? If you were *just friends* with a guy, there's no way you'd walk around holding his hand. It's not what friends do."

"Well, I told you Royal liked you. You're just hard headed."

Gemma grinned and then glanced towards the house. "Uh, oh. Your man's coming."

Gianna looked up and saw Ramsey walking toward the car. "He probably thinks something's wrong since we're just sitting in the car."

"Yep, and let me say this real quick before he gets over here. I know I joke about you two kissing and being all lovey-dovey, but I adore the way he loves you."

"Aw..." Gianna smiled. "You could have that, too, if you stop pretending you and Royal are *just friends*. It's okay if you like him."

"Why thank you, mother," Gemma quipped. "I'll call him up right now and ask if we can go steady."

Gianna chuckled. "Very funny."

When Ramsey was a few steps away from the car, Gianna opened the door and said, "Hey, Ramsey."

"Hey," he said, reaching for her hand to help

her out of the car like it was necessary. He glanced over at Gemma at the same time.

"Hey, Gem."

"Hey."

"Is everything okay?" he asked.

"Yeah," Gianna said. "We were just sitting here having a lil' girl chat. That's all."

"Oh. I see. Then, pardon my interruption."

"No worries," Gemma said. "I'm sure Gianna isn't done with me yet."

Gianna smiled while Gemma continued walking to the house.

Chapter 10

Gemma took a warm bath and massaged her feet after being on them nearly all day. Then she slid into a thin, see-through nightshirt and sat on the bed. She brushed her naturally curly hair before securing it in the scarf, then checked her phone when she saw the indicator light flashing. She'd missed a call from somebody and she had a clue who that somebody was. Royal. He'd called thirty minutes ago and ten minutes ago, he sent a text:

Royal: I was calling to say goodnight, but you
        must be snoozing already :-(
Royal: sweet dreams, diamond

She smiled, wondering if she should call him back or let him think she was sleep. But like a giddy schoolgirl, she couldn't bear the thought of not calling him so she dialed his number.

"Gemma?" he answered.

"Yeah, it's me. I just got your text messages."

"And here I was thinking you were sleeping already."

"No. I was taking a bath when you called and I spent fifteen minutes massaging my feet. It's tough standing up all day. I don't see how Gianna does it."

"You should've called me earlier. I would've come over and rubbed your feet."

Gemma laughed. "Your hands are not coming nowhere near my feet. Plus, I took care of it, so..."

"I was waiting for you to call me today. I told you I would pick you up from the bakery if you got tired."

"I know. I just didn't want to leave Gianna there by herself. But I'm not going tomorrow, so I get to sleep for as long as I want."

"Good. You deserve it."

"You can say that again."

"So, do you know all about baking cupcakes now?"

Gemma grinned. "I know how to make the batter, and it's not as easy as you think. Baking is hard, tedious work."

"I'm sure it is."

"Everything has to be measured just right. But, it's fun watching Gianna do it. She's a pro. I bet my niece, or nephew, is going to be born knowing how to whip up some cupcakes."

Royal chuckled. "Probably."

"So, how was your day, Royal?"

"My day?" he asked.

"Yeah. What did you do all day?"

"Uh...I spent most of the day looking for new vendors for a project we've been working on."

"What kind of project?"

"A European style building in Uptown. Construction hasn't started yet, but we want to make sure we have all the vendors in place for when it does."

"Sounds serious."

"It is, but it'll get handled. Have you taken your medicine yet?"

"I have, so you can rest easy knowing I'm going to be okay."

"I would rest a lot easier if I could see that for myself."

"Or, you can just take my word for it."

"I still would like to see you, though," he confessed.

Gemma nervously chewed on her bottom lip as she listened to the relaxed, sexy drawl of his voice. "Why?"

"Because you were here all weekend and now, I'm lying in bed alone, visualizing your pretty face in my mind when I could be looking at it instead. When I could be brushing my thumb across those beautiful freckles on your face."

"Stop flirting with me, Royal. I'm not one of your women."

"*One* of my women?" He chuckled. "I don't have any women."

"Sure you don't," Gemma said. Everywhere they went together, women were checking him out.

"What do you have planned for tomorrow besides sleeping?" he asked.

"I'm going to call the hospital to inquire about volunteering."

"Oh, that's right. You told me that."

"Yep, and I'll be studying for my driver's

license."

"What if the hospital asks you to come up there?" he asked.

"They probably won't but if they do, I'll get Carson to take me."

"Carson?"

"Yeah. He already told me he'd be my chauffer if I needed to go anywhere."

"That's nice of him, but tell the old man to lean back. If you need to go somewhere, I'll take you."

"How, Royal? You *do* have a job."

"So does he."

"Okay, you have a point, but running errands is a part of Carson's job."

"I suppose so."

"Anyway, I'm going to let you go to bed," Gemma said, yawning.

"You're going to let *me* go to bed," Royal said, then chuckled.

"Yeah, and for future reference, don't you ever in your life send me a sad face emoji."

He grinned. "What's wrong with the sad face? That is how I was feeling when you didn't answer your phone."

Gemma rolled her eyes. "Whatever, Royal."

"And I'll send you all the emojis I want to send. As a matter of fact, I'm going to buy you one of those emoji pillows just for that. Every time you look at it, you'll think of me."

Laughing, Gemma said, "You better not step up in here with an emoji pillow. I dare you."

"Oh, then it's already done."

"Seriously, Royal?"

"Yeah. You can't dare me not to do something, especially when it relates to you."

"Oh, gosh. I'll keep that in mind. Now, get off this phone and go to bed. You have to work in the morning."

"I got another meeting with my brothers first thing in the morning. I suppose I should get some sleep. I need to be well-rested to deal with them."

"Then, yes, get some sleep."

"Alright. Well, goodnight, diamond girl."

"There you go with that again. Why do you call me that? It sounds like a stripper name."

Royal laughed. "I can assure you, it's not a stripper name, girl, at least in the context I'm using it in."

"And what context is that?"

"A diamond is a gem. *Gem* is your nickname. That's why I call you my diamond girl."

My diamond girl...

"Aw...now it sounds sweet."

"Then that makes it the perfect nickname for you."

Gemma smiled so wide, her face could hardly contain it. "Goodnight, Royal."

"Sweet dreams," he said, then hung up the phone.

Gemma fell back on the bed, reeling in happiness while her heart pattered with excitement. What if Gianna was right all along? What if Royal really was into her?

Chapter 11

"You'll be happy to know that we already got the approval from this great city of Charlotte, North Carolina to build the Paris structure at the designated site in Uptown," Romulus said, in a good mood as he stepped into Ramsey's office where his brothers had assembled.

"Is that why you're skipping around this morning?" Royal asked, taking a sip of coffee, still having trouble waking himself up after not getting much sleep last night. Every time he closed his eyes to rest, there was an image of her – Gemma – popping up in his head, forcing him to daydream about her rather than sleep. And last night, while he laid on the bed, staring up at the ceiling, he thought about how it would feel to kiss her – not those little innocent kisses he'd leave on her temple or cheek every once in a while. He wanted one that wasn't so innocent. A wild, untamed one. How would she react to being kissed since he knew she'd never been kissed before? Never been touched. Never been served up a dose of love by any means. He desperately wanted to love her in every sense of the word. But how could he do that when, in her mind, he was only a friend?

"You look like crap, Royal," Regal commented.

"That's exactly how I feel." Royal took a sip of black coffee.

"Late night?" Romulus asked.

"Yeah," Royal said. "Something like that."

Ramsey frowned. Just a couple of days ago, Royal was professing his love for Gemma, and now he was having a 'late night' hangover? That was precisely the kind of behavior he didn't like when it came to his brother. One minute, he was into a girl and the next, he was feeling someone else. Had he not warned Royal? Instead of broaching the subject in front of his brothers, he steered toward the business of Paris. "Regal will be in Paris next week, meeting with Basile. I'll be video conferencing with them along with the rest of team. Royal, I think it would be a good idea for you to go along with Regal."

Royal didn't like the sound of that one bit. "Why?"

To get you away from my sister-in-law. You can have all the late nights you want there. "You said we were having vendor trouble. While you're with Regal in Paris, you can spend your time meeting with potential vendors."

"Are you telling me you want overseas vendors for this project?" Royal asked.

"Yes. I would like to explore the—"

"The last time I brought the idea of overseas vendors to you, you nearly popped a blood vessel. Now, all of a sudden, it's a good idea, huh?"

"Man...here we go," Regal said, reclining back in his chair.

"Yes, it's a good idea," Ramsey said, glaring at his brother.

"Why? Because *you* thought of it?" Royal asked angrily. Having to go to Paris for a week meant he couldn't see Gemma for a week and that pissed him off to no end.

"No, not because I thought of it. It's what needs to be done," Ramsey snapped. "If you don't like it, Royal, go do something else and I'll hire somebody who can get the job done."

"Whoa, alright let's take it down a notch," Romulus said, attempting to establish peace between his quarreling brothers.

Royal wasn't interested. He stood up and not only left the office, but he had to get out of the building. He took the elevator down to the ground floor and paced the sidewalk in front of SCA's headquarters. Lack of sleep and having to put up with Ramsey so early in the morning turned out to be the perfect storm for some nonsense. He could only hope Gemma's day was turning out to be a lot better than his.

* * *

Gemma took Gianna's laptop to the kitchen and looked up the number to the children's cancer center. She dialed the number to the volunteer office and waited anxiously for someone to pick up. When she finally heard the voice of a woman, she said, "Hi. I'm looking for some information about your volunteer program."

"Have you volunteered with us or any of our affiliates before?"

"No. This would be the first time."

"And is this for school credit or—"

"No. It would be just for the sake of volunteering. I'm a cancer survivor and so I know what it's like to face that. To feel hopeless. My goal is to use my story to inspire others."

"Ah, I see. Well, congratulations on winning your battle, dear."

"Thank you."

"And as for becoming a volunteer, you would first have to fill out our online application. Once we review it and determine you're a good fit for a volunteer position, you would have to have a background check and drug test. When you pass those, we'll call you to arrange a possible volunteer schedule."

"Perfect."

"Do you need the link to the online application?"

"No, ma'am. I'm actually looking at it right now."

"Okay, good. I look forward to seeing your application. What was your name again?"

"Gemma Jacobsen."

"It was nice talking to you, Gemma."

"It was nice talking to you as well."

"Bye, now."

"Bye."

Gemma hung up the phone, then jumped off

of the barstool and shook her butt while waving her arms in the air.

"Do you need medical attention, madam?" Carson asked with a smirk on his face.

"Ha, ha, ha, very funny, Carson." She and Carson had grown close over the last couple of months, so much so that she'd go to him for advice on some things – stuff she couldn't ask her father. How could she when she didn't know who her father was or if he was still alive? She contemplated talking to Geraldine about it but talked herself out of it just as easily.

"I take it you're happy about something," Carson said.

"Yes. I just spoke with a representative at the children's hospital. If all goes well, you are looking at the newest volunteer, my friend."

"Wonderful. I hope all goes well."

"Thank you, Carson."

"You're welcome."

Carson opened the refrigerator and seemed to be studying its contents.

"What are you up to today?" she asked him.

"Nothing but making sure the St. Claire Estate is operating efficiently."

"You're really good at your job, by the way. I don't know what Ramsey would do without you here running things."

"That's sweet of you to say."

"And I mean it. I want to be as good as you at something."

Carson closed the refrigerator and looked at the big, light brown eyes beaming back at him. She wanted to talk. He wanted to be available to listen. "You will be. You're young. What are you? Seven?"

She cackled. "I'm twenty, silly."

"I know. I was just teasing. Compared to me, you're incredibly young. You have your whole life ahead of you to be *good* at something. Don't make the mistake of putting undue pressure on yourself, madam. Take life one day at a time."

Gemma smiled as Carson looked inside the refrigerator again and took down some notes.

"I have to run out to get some groceries and supplies," he said. "Do you need anything?"

"No. I'm good."

"Will you be okay by yourself for a couple of hours?"

"Yeah. I'll be fine."

"Alright. If you need me, just ring my cell."

"Will do."

Gemma returned to the barstool where she'd been sitting and clicked on the volunteer application. She was getting ready to fill it out when she had a sudden desire to call Royal. She usually didn't bother him during the day since he was at work, but today, she had a hankering to call. She dialed his number, waited for a moment and finally, on the fourth ring, she heard his voice when he asked, "Why are you calling me?"

His questioned stunned her for a moment. He sounded upset. "I was just calling to say hi. If it's a bad time—"

"No, it's not a bad time."

"Then why do you sound upset?"

"Because I *am* upset."

"What happened?"

"It's nothing for you to concern yourself with."

"Okay. That's going to be my response to you the next time you ask me how I'm feeling. Or if I took my medication. Or why my day was sucky."

"Don't start with me, Gemma."

"Talk to me, then." When he didn't say anything she sang out, "I'm waiting..."

"It..." he released a heavy sigh. "Me and Ramsey got into it again. That's all."

"Should've known...hope you two can work it out."

"We always do. It's just the process of working it out that irks me the most but forget all that. What have you been up to today?"

"I'm trying to fill out this application for the hospital."

"For the volunteer gig?"

"Yep...called and talked to the coordinator this morning."

"Good. Is Carson taking care of you?"

"Of course. He ran out to do some shopping."

"Wait...so you're there alone?"

Gemma could hear the panic in his voice. "Yes, I'm here alone and there's no reason for you to be alarmed because I'm fine."

Royal didn't respond.

Gemma took his silence as worry or strategizing. "I'm fine, Royal," Gemma said again. "Don't try to come up with some inventive way to troubleshoot this. I'm okay. Okay?"

"Okay," he said.

"Let me hear you smile."

"What are you talking about, girl?" he asked.

"I want to hear you smile," she told him. "Release the frustration and show me those pearly whites."

Royal grinned. "You're not even here to see them."

"I can see them in my mind. Now, make sure you talk to Ramsey before you leave. I don't know why you two are always getting into it."

Because he's trying to keep me away from you. That's why. "I'll talk to him. I don't want you there worrying about me, Gemma."

"Sorry. Now that I know your big head, I can't help but worry about you, *your majesty.*"

He grinned again. "Speaking of *knowing* me, it's about time for us to have one of those in-depth one-on-ones."

"Why do you have to make it sound like therapy?"

"Ay, by the time I'm finished with you, there may be some psychological benefits. I know it will certainly help me figure out why I can't stop thinking about you."

"What?" she asked. Had she heard him correctly? "What'd you say?"

"I have to go, Gem. I'll call you later."

"Okay. Bye."

"Bye," Gemma said slowly, placing her phone on the countertop next to the laptop. Did he...? Did he really just say what she thought he'd said?

Chapter 12

Near the end of the workday, after he thought Royal may have cooled down (but it really didn't faze him if he had or hadn't), Ramsey walked to Royal's office and took a seat. Royal, glanced up from his computer for a second to see Ramsey sitting, but then he looked at his computer screen again. He did an Internet search for emoji pillows and found the sad-faced one. He smirked. It was a joke between himself and Gemma and since she dared him not to, he just *had* to buy it. He leaned over to take his wallet from his back right pocket then pulled out a credit card. His plan was to have the pillow shipped overnight directly to her.

"I warned you not to hurt her," Ramsey said.

Royal glanced up at Ramsey again, frowned, but continued keying in his credit card number. "I have no idea what you're talking about."

"Man, Royal, you came up in here this morning, bragging about having a late night."

"I wasn't bragging," Royal said, selecting the 'next day' delivery option.

"That's what it sounded like to me. You don't know what you want, do you?" Ramsey asked.

"That's always been your problem."

Royal closed his laptop and reached for the laptop bag next to his desk. He unzipped it. "You've managed to irritate me this morning, Ram. I'm not going to let you do it again."

"Here's what I don't understand," Ramsey continued. "If you haven't gotten all those player ways out of your system, what are you doing confessing—more like claiming—that you love Gemma."

Royal zipped up his bag. "I *do* love Gemma."

"So, let me get this straight. You love Gemma, but you're still messing around with other women?"

Royal looked up and saw the frown on his brother's face. How could he be mad when it was obvious Ramsey had Gemma's back? Had the utmost concern for her. That meant he and his brother were on the same team, right? The only problem was, Ramsey made some assumptions about what he thought Royal's 'late night' comment had meant. Royal decided it was time to clarify, but calmly. "Ram, calm down." Royal smiled. "When I said I had a *late night*, did it ever occur to you that I could've had a late night with Gemma?"

"Gemma was home last night."

"She was, and I was on the phone with her," Royal explained. "When I got off the phone with her last night, I couldn't sleep because I couldn't stop thinking about her. I'm not messing around with other women. I told you, Ramsey, I love Gemma and I would never do anything to hurt her. That's why I was pissed that you're sending me to Paris. How am I supposed to see her from Paris? How do I make sure she's okay and keep in touch with the time zone difference and all?"

Ramsey's expression softened. Now, he understood Royal's frustration. His little brother was in love. In love with Gemma. He smiled. "Wow. You really love her, don't you?"

"I do, and it's nothing forced. Nothing that I'm making myself do. I care about her and being with her, helping her recover, checking on her, buying food for her, taking care of her is like second nature to me. The only thing I fear is something happening to her."

"Gemma will be fine, and I hate to tell you this, but you do still need to go to Paris. We need to get a handle on this vendor issue before it becomes an even bigger problem."

Royal pulled in a breath, then replied, "That's fine. All I ask is that Gemma is taken care of while I'm gone. The first inkling I get that she's sick or something's wrong, I'm on the first flight back. That, I can promise you."

Ramsey smiled. "Don't worry. She'll be in good hands while you're working."

"She better be," he said, then took his bag and walked out of the office.

Chapter 13

Later that evening, after stuffing herself with some of Carson's homemade alfredo, Gemma put on a sweater and went outside. She reclined in a chair by the pool and let her eyes drift with the water on the chilly evening that quickly became night. The outside lights were already illuminating and there was a dampness in the air like it was due to rain. But it was nice and being out here gave her time to think. She didn't do a lot of reflecting in the past since she didn't think she needed to, but now that the future looked bright, she was finding herself wanting answers.

Like Gianna, she wanted to know why their mother, Geraldine, abandoned them. Why didn't she bother with trying to ensure she got the proper care she needed when she was younger? Who knows? Had Geraldine actually been a mother and taken care of her children, maybe the doctors would've found the cancer sooner in which case, she could've possibly been spared all the subsequent pain of chemo and the uphill battle of recovery. And she still had no idea who her father was. Was he still alive? Did he want to have a relationship with her? Or did he not know she existed? She'd learned from Gianna that Geraldine didn't even tell Gianna's father, Jerome, that he had a daughter. What if her father didn't know about her?

Then there was her future to contemplate. What did she want to do with her life? Volunteering was a good start, but at some point, she wanted to be independent. To take care of herself. She couldn't take care of herself without making money and while volunteering was rewarding in itself, it certainly wouldn't pay any bills.

And then there was Royal...

She wasn't hearing things today. He actually said he couldn't stop thinking about her, but then again, if she was being honest with herself, Royal always said something flirtatious whenever he came around her. But it seemed to be happening more frequently to be mere coincidences. No, he was doing this intentionally. But why?

"Hey, Gem," Gianna said, breaking into her thoughts.

Gemma looked up at her sister and smiled. "Hey."

"Slide over so I can sit down."

"Gianna, there are a million chairs out here and you want to sit next to me?"

"Yes. Now slide your skinny butt over."

Gemma moved over enough to give Gianna clearance to recline beside her.

"Ah," Gianna said. "Me and baby sis...just like old times."

"Oh, crap. Please tell me you're not going down memory lane again."

Gianna laughed. "No. It's just crazy how different life is now. When people say your life can change in the blink of an eye, I know exactly what they mean."

"Yeah. You met your prince charming and now you're living your happily ever after."

"Not only that but think about everything else that's changed, Gemma. You are better now, thank God. We don't have to struggle anymore. The bakery is doing outstanding. My nerves are under control—well partially. Ramsey still makes me—"

"La, la, la," Gemma said covering her ears. "Nobody wants to know what Ramsey does to you. Keep that to yourself."

Gianna laughed. "Anyway, my point is, we've come a long way."

"We have. I still need to figure out what I want though. After having conversations with Royal, I realize I want more for myself. I want to know why mom is such a nutcase. Or if she really *is* a nutcase. I want to know if she actually has legitimate reasons for leaving us."

"Well, I can save you some time there, Gem. She's already told—"

"I know what she told you but I feel like I need to talk to her personally to see where her head is at."

Gianna nodded. She could understand that even though she knew what the outcome would be. Geraldine had some serious issues, and surely Gemma would see that for herself if she decided to meet with her.

"And I want to know if I have a father," Gemma continued.

"You deserve to know those things, Gem. I wish I could've found those answers for you."

"You've done enough for me, Gianna. I'm getting better now. It's time I start doing some things for myself."

"Have you been studying for your driver's test?"

"I have. I've decided that I'm going to take my time because I only want to take this test once. I've heard horror stories about the DMV."

"Oh yeah," Gianna chuckled. "You don't want to get stuck at the DMV. I'd rather eat a gallon of cottage cheese than make that mistake."

"But you hate cottage cheese."

"That's the point I'm trying to make."

Gemma chuckled, then stared up at the star-sprinkled night sky. "I'm surprised your husband ain't out here looking for you yet."

"That's because I told him I was coming out here to check on you."

"Oh." Gemma released a breath. "So, I have a confession to make."

"And what might that be?"

"Um…" She was too nervous to say it at first, then she blurted out, "I think you were right about…"

"What?"

"Royal."

"In what aspect?"

"That he likes me."

"Aw shucky duck," Gianna said.

Gemma laughed. "The expression is *shucky ducky*, Gianna."

"Whatever. I told you Royal liked you! He's been feeling you since *forever*."

"No, he hasn't. In the beginning, there was a clear distinction of us being friends. Now, I don't know. He's always saying things—like how beautiful I am, and how he can't stop thinking about me."

Gianna's eyebrows raised toward her hairline. "He actually said that to you?"

"He told me he couldn't stop thinking about me when I talked to him earlier. I think it slipped out though because shortly after he said it, he found a reason to get off of the phone."

"Jeez, Louise! And I thought Ramsey was bold. I had known him for all of two days when he sucked chocolate off of my finger. Now, he licks it off of anyplace he—"

"La, la, la....oh, my poor ears," Gemma said.

Gianna giggled.

"Ramsey turned you into a lil' freak, huh?"

"No. It's just what lovers do," Gianna explained. "But I don't have to explain. You'll find out soon enough. Royal's flavor of choice might be caramel. You know it takes longer to lick off caramel."

Gemma looked at Gianna and said, "If you weren't pregnant, I'd push you right off of this chair."

Gianna couldn't stop chuckling, placing a hand on her stomach as she did so. "Karma is so sweet," she said. "Remember when you used to tease me about Ramsey liking me? Huh? Now, it's payback time! Royal likes you and you don't know how to take it."

"I don't know how to take it because I could never see anyone falling in love with me. I mean, not to say that Royal is falling in love with me...I'm just sayin'. I never imagined a man finding me interesting, especially one like him."

"He's never told you that he loves you?"

"Well, yeah, but it's in a friendly way like, *love ya, girl*. You know. It's not like the dreamy-eyed love. The kind of love like when Ramsey looks at you. I can see love in his eyes and all up in his facial expressions when he looks at you. I don't see that when Royal looks at me. Maybe it's there. Maybe it's not. I don't know. I never had it. Never experienced it, so how would I know?"

"Well, let's look at the facts. First of all, he always wants to be with you. Second, I've watched him, on several occasions stare you down when you weren't looking. He likes to steal eye shots of you when you're unaware."

"Gosh...that's so nerve-racking."

"Why?"

"Because half the time, I look a hot mess. I have no figure so I don't even know what he's looking at."

"You *do* have a body. Listen...if a man *really* likes you, which we already know Royal does, he'll be more focused on the person you are on the inside instead of the outside."

Gemma nodded, then pulled her phone from the right pocket of her sweater when she felt it vibrating. She looked at the display and said, "Oh, shoot. It's Royal."

"Welp, that's my cue," Gianna said standing up. "I don't want you to catch a cold, so don't stay out here too much longer, okay."

"I won't."

She waited until Gianna was a good distance away before answering the phone. "Hello."

"What you mean, *hello*? You know who this is?"

Gemma gnawed on her bottom lip as she listened to the sexy tone of his voice again. "How are you tonight, Royal?" she asked. Conversing with him seemed a lot different now that she had reason to believe he was feeling her.

"I'm good, but I'd be a lot better if I was there. With you."

She smiled, letting his words float around in her mind. When she settled back down to earth, she heard him ask, "What are you up to?"

"I'm sitting outside by the pool."

"It's not raining there?"

"No."

"It's pouring down over here," Royal said.

"Seriously?"

"Yep."

"That's crazy. I wish it was raining here. I love the rain."

"I do, too," Royal said. "It does something to me."

Gemma chuckled. "You mean like when the old people say it messes with their arthritis?"

"No."

"Then how?"

"It turns me on. Don't ask why. It just does."

"Oh," Gemma said, deciding she wasn't going to ask him a thing more about being *turned on* or nothing else related to his desires.

"I wish you were here," he told her.

She swallowed the lump in her throat. He wished she was there after he just admitted to being *turned on* by the rain? Is that what he said? Yeah, that's what he said. She was sure of it. But just to make sure, she asked, "What'd you say?"

"I said, I wished you were here."

"Uh..." She swallowed hard. Okay, she'd heard him correctly. Why did his voice have to sound extra smooth and delicious though? Jeez. "You—you said you wish I was there?"

"Yes. That's what I said, Gemma. Is something wrong with your phone?"

She could hear a slight chuckle come across the line when she asked, "Why do you wish I was there?"

"Because I miss you. I haven't seen you all day. I hate not being able to see you. Hate it."

A chill or something like it ran through her bones. "I missed you too, Royal."

"No, you didn't," he teased.

She laughed. "I did."

"What'd you miss about me?"

"That ginormous bear hug you usually give me."

"That's it? You miss my body?"

"That's not what I said."

"It is. You miss my body," he joked. "Admit it."

"I will admit no such a thing, silly," Gemma said, tickled. "Anyway, did you get things ironed out with Ramsey? I know you were a lil' upset earlier."

"Yes. I think he understands me now." *Understands how much I love you.*

"Good. I'm glad everything worked out."

"Me, too. On another note, looks like I'll be heading to Paris for a week."

Gemma frowned. "You—you're going to Paris for a whole week?"

"Yes, unfortunately. Me and Regal will be flying out Monday morning."

"Oh," Gemma said trying to keep the disappointment out of her voice. The knowledge of knowing she wouldn't see Royal for a week was disappointing. She wondered if she'd get a chance to spend some time with him before he left.

"Gem?"

"I'm here. I was just thinking."

"About what?"

"You leaving. I don't know if I like that, Royal."

"I know. I don't like it either, but it'll go by fast."

"Can you at least come by and say goodbye to me, first?"

"Gemma, I'm not leaving until Monday, bae."

"I know, but—" she sighed, but her heart was constantly racing.

"Talk to me, Gem."

"Okay. Tomorrow's Wednesday. As it stands, I haven't seen you at all today and I—I just—when am I going to see you again?"

"You sound panicky. Stop it."

"So, I'm not supposed to care, Royal?"

"That's not what I'm saying. I—"

"Then when am I going to see you again?" she asked. She didn't care that she sounded needy and desperate because she *was* those things. She'd grown close to Royal and was used to having him around and now, he was going to be gone for an entire week? What was she going to do without him for a week, especially after they'd been inseparable for three months? "You know what. Forget it. I'm trippin'. I'm sure you'll show up whenever you get ready, so—"

"*Do not* hang up on me, Gemma."

"Then say goodnight to me and I won't have to."

Silence.

Long, awkward, painful silence.

Royal wasn't about to say goodnight and influenced by the austerity of his warning tone, Gemma wasn't about to hang up. So the silence lengthened. Grew. One minute. Then two. Then...

"Okay. I don't like where this conversation is headed," Royal said, "So before either of us say something we don't mean, I think it'll be best to end it."

End it. End what? The conversation? The friendship? Gemma was so angry, she had no clue what he meant. She just wanted to hurry up and get off of the phone.

Royal continued, "So, I'm going to say goodnight, and—"

"Goodnight," she responded quickly right before hanging up the phone. She stood up and walked toward the house. What the heck just happened? One minute, she was on cloud nine telling her sister how she thought Royal liked her and the next, she was abruptly ending a phone call with him and feeling bad for doing so. And he was going away to Paris for a week. That's what really bothered her. For the first time during the course of their friendship, she was forced to recognize that he held all the cards when it came to *them*. The only time she saw him was when he made himself available to see her. When he drove over to Ramsey's house or came by to pick her up to take her to the movies or out to grab a bite to eat. He held the cards, and she didn't like that one bit. Never before did she need her independence more than she needed it right now. But one just couldn't be independent without a driver's license and a job. That's what she needed to focus on instead of sweating a man who may or may not want her.

Chapter 14

Gemma clicked the submit button, successfully submitting her application. She folded the laptop closed then looked at the driver's handbook. She was beyond tired with just doing that task. She had no energy left to study. She needed to be wide awake and refreshed before trying to learn about *right of ways* and the meaning of double yellow center lines.

"You have a package, madam," Carson said, stepping into the kitchen, carrying a box.

"I do?" Gemma asked, looking up at him as he brought a medium-sized box into the kitchen.

"Yes. Would you like for me to open it for you?"

"Oh, no, Carson. I can open a box, but thank you."

"You're welcome." Carson placed the box on the counter, in arm's reach of her. "Is everything okay by the way? I noticed you looked a little down at breakfast this morning."

"Oh, it's nothing," she said dismissively.

"Nothing, you say? I didn't know Royal went by the nickname *nothing* these days...learn something new every day, I reckon."

Gemma glanced up at him. She knew he was a wise man, but a mind reader, too? "How'd you know it's about Royal?"

"I would say lucky guess, but I know better. *Nothing* calls me every single day to check up on you."

"He does?"

"Yes, indeed. Sometimes multiple times a day."

"You're kidding."

"Not this time, madam."

Still not believing a word he said, she asked, "How long has this been going on?"

Carson chuckled. "You make it sound like a conspiracy."

"It is...somebody's doing something behind my back. Isn't that like...wrong on so many levels?"

"Not when what's being done behind your back is in your best interest, dear."

I guess it wouldn't be, Gemma surmised. "So tell me...how long has he been checking up on me behind my back?"

The old man couldn't get the amusement off of his face. "For quite a while."

"How long is a while?"

"Since you were released from the hospital after your surgery, madam. Just yesterday he called and chewed me out about leaving you here alone. You must've told him I ran out to do some shopping."

"I mentioned it casually when I spoke with him, yes, but I didn't think he was mad about it, and I definitely didn't think he would call to fuss at you."

"Well, let me tell you...I had to hold the phone away from my ear."

"It was *that* bad?"

"Yes. That bad."

"Carson, please accept my apology on his behalf. He gets too protective of me and sometimes, he doesn't know when to take a step back."

"No, it's alright. It's fine by me. I can't be mad at the man for showing how much he loves his woman."

"Ah...uh...um, I'm sorry." She shook her head as if to physically juggle her thoughts together. "What was that?"

"I said, Royal loves you. You *do* know that, right?"

"Um..." Gemma scratched her head. "He gets on my nerves, Carson, like really, really bad."

Carson smiled. "That's only because you love him, too."

"Ugh...love, love, love. Why does everyone keep tossing this word around like it's disposable?"

"It's not disposable. It's liberating. It's what people live for. What people *long* for and if you're lucky enough to find it, and by all accounts, you have been, then you better hang on to it."

"Carson, did you not hear what I just told you? Royal get's on my nerves."

Carson laughed harder. "Oh, young love. I remember those days. Boy, I tell ya..."

Gemma looked at the man like he was crazy. Was he not listening to her or what? He seemed to be in dreamland. Reminiscing about when he was younger and whatnot.

Before she could offer another complaint about Royal, Carson said, "I lost my wife a long time ago. What I wouldn't give to have an argument with her now..."

He set about his business and she sat there thinking about what it was he was trying to relay to her. Dang it, she hated it when people made her see a point. Made her see the importance of loving people while they were still here because tomorrow isn't promised and all that jazz.

But who knew that better than her? There were many days when she thought her tomorrows would be nonexistent. When she felt like her life was ending – a horrible feeling for a young woman. A horrible feeling for anyone. But just because she couldn't predict the future – did that mean she wasn't entitled to her feelings? She felt like she was, and her feelings had her upset with Royal at the moment but more so at herself. She wanted independence. She wanted her life to start right now. Not later. She'd *waited* enough. She was tired of waiting.

And then there was all this talk about Royal being in love with her. Gianna had tried convincing her that Royal loved her and now, Carson had reiterated those same sentiments. It all confused Gemma because since they were assuming it, now her mind wanted to believe that Royal was falling in love with her. But, what if they were wrong?

They probably were. Royal liked to flirt. He was a ladies man. He had started out being all touchy-feely with her. Even when she was lying in the hospital bed after her surgery, she'd wake up to him holding her, massaging her fingers or gently brushing the side of his face against hers to gauge her body temperature. That was normal for him, but everyone was interpreting it for more than what it was. They had to have been because if he was all that worried about her – and *that* much into her – why was he hightailing it to Paris?

She held her temples, then said, "Ugh, get out of my head."

She stood up from the barstool and filled a glass with tap water. While she sipped, she looked at the box that Carson had placed on the counter. She frowned. *What the heck is that?*

She set the glass by the sink, then ripped off some of the packing tape from the box and after some tugging, she finally got it open, removing a round, yellow pillow. A sad-face, emoji pillow. If she wasn't irritated and pissed at Royal at the moment, she would've found it hilarious. But since Royal was leaving in a few days, she wasn't so much in a playful mood. She had to do something to get her mind off of him – hard to do since he was all she could think about. And now this pillow...

Do something, Gemma. Do something to get your mind off of him. She thought about taking a nap, but he'd probably pop up in her dreams somewhere – that's if she could get to sleep. She sighed, looked at her phone and decided to call Gianna.

"The Boardwalk Bakery. How can I help you?"

"Hey, Gianna, baby," Gemma said, trying to imitate Ramsey's deep voice. "I want some cupcakes."

Gianna laughed. "Why are you calling me on the business phone, Gem? You used to call me on my cell phone."

"Okay, Drake," Gemma quipped.

"Huh?" Gianna asked, not catching the Drake reference.

"Ugh...whatever. Anyway, what's up? What'cha doing?"

"I'm super busy today...finally getting around to baking cupcakes for St. Claire Architects. Judy will be here any minute to pick them up."

"Who's Judy?"

"Ramsey's executive assistant."

"Oh."

"What are you doing? Are you studying for your driver's test?"

"Nope. I'm too tired to be looking at this complicated book. It's too much. Left signal. Right signal. Yield. U-turns. Ugh. It never ends. And why do you have to stop for school buses?"

"So you don't mow down people's kids. That's why you have to stop, silly." Gianna laughed. "Look, you can't be out here breaking the rules of the road. Your lil' butt gon' be sitting behind bars."

"I feel like I'm already behind bars. I can't go anywhere. I have to wait for people to come and see me."

"People like who? Royal?"

"Don't even get started on Royal. He's all everybody wants to talk about. Royal, Royal, Royal, Royal, Royal—"

"Gemma?"

"Royal, Royal, Royal, Royal, Royal."

"Gemma Jacobsen?" Gianna said trying to get her attention again.

"What?"

"Okay. I won't talk about Royal, but when you say you have to wait for people to come and see you, who are you referring to?"

Royal. She wasn't about to admit that, though, so she said, "I just want to be able to go when I want to go. Right now, I'm stuck."

"Okay, Gem...first, you have to take your health into consideration. I know you're feeling better and all but you had a major surgery, baby girl. You don't need to be running all around town. And that reminds me—you have the appointment tomorrow. Is Royal still taking you because—?"

"No. I want you to take me."

"You cut me off before I could finish. I've already made commitments for tomorrow since you said Royal was taking you to the doctor. I have four catering orders and—"

"Okay. Okay. Fine."

"Why don't you want him to take you?" Gianna inquired.

"I just don't—I...nevermind. Get back to

work. I'll talk to you later."

"Okay. Call me if you need anything."

"Yep. Bye." As she hung up the phone, Royal was calling. Gemma just stared at the display and said, "Nope. I'm not going to do it," she said. After the intense conversation they had on the phone last night, she didn't want to talk to him just yet. She was still irritated. During the last ring, she mumbled, "Just go to Paris and leave me alone...you and your stupid emoji pillow."

Carson walked by when she made the statement and said, "Young love."

Gemma rolled her eyes, then got up off of the stool and snatched the driver's handbook off of the counter. She went upstairs, to her room and closed the door. She yawned as she tossed the book onto her nightstand and fell across the bed, long overdue for an afternoon nap.

Chapter 15

"Not eating in the dining room with Ramsey and Gianna today I see," Carson said.

"Oh, don't start with me, Carson."

"Just making an observation," Carson said after noticing she'd been in her room for the entire afternoon and didn't bother coming out, even when she knew Gianna was home.

"Yeah, I figured I'd eat in the kitchen to give Gianna and Ramsey time to talk about their married-life stuff without third-wheel-Gemma awkwardly rolling around." She propped her head up on her hands.

"I'm sure they don't see it that way," Carson said preparing a plate for her.

She didn't care if they did or didn't. She wasn't in the mood to be around the mushy love that always accumulated in the air whenever Gianna and Ramsey were within a few feet of each other. Not this evening.

"Here you go, madam," Carson said sitting the plate down in front of her. "Beef tips over rice with steamed broccoli and a yeast roll."

"It smells good, Carson. Thank you."

"You're welcome. Eat up," Carson said, and then he quickly left the kitchen, hurrying to the front door since the bell had chimed, its orchestra-like tone filling the house as thoroughly as the food aroma had.

Gemma got up, walked over to the refrigerator and took out a carton of orange juice. She filled a glass with ice. Then she sat down again and poured herself a full glass of juice. After taking a long sip, she tasted the beef tips but soon lowered her fork. She could've sworn she heard Royal's voice coming from the dining room, but then again, he and his brothers sounded alike. Maybe it was her mind wishing it was him while at the same time dreading seeing him. How twisty was that? To wish to see someone, yet not actually *want* to see them?

"There's my girl," Royal said with confidence as he stepped into the kitchen.

Gemma glanced over to the sound of his voice. Dang. It *was* him! Had she known he was coming over, she would've taken her dinner to go – and by *to go*, she meant locked inside of her bedroom. Instead, she had her tall, bearded, wildly exotic *friend* walking toward her, dressed in a pair of blue, ribbed-panel, distressed fabric jeans that fit his laid-back, off-work swag perfectly and a white T-shirt. He wore a Carolina blue baseball cap turned to the back that made him look more like his age although the beard offset it with a more mature look.

She hoped he wasn't coming directly for her – like for a hug or some other display of affection that he took it upon himself to take from her. Maybe he'd just sit down. And stare. *Crap.* She didn't want that either. That would be much worse. She couldn't handle much more of his staring or nothing else, especially tonight. *Why did you have to come here tonight?*

Sure enough, in true Royal fashion, he walked right up to her and leaned down to place a kiss at her temple, but Gemma ducked away from his lips. *This* time.

He frowned but quickly shook it off since he already knew she was upset. Dealing with a woman and her *feelings* would take some getting used to. He certainly wasn't comfortable with her mood swings to something he considered to be minor. But what was minor to him could've been something major for her. Was she really upset about him going to Paris, or was it something else? And why did she have to look so pretty when she was mad with her cute, little pouty lips and flushed, freckled cheeks?

"So, you're still mad at me, huh?"

"I'm just trying to enjoy my dinner," she said curtly.

Royal stepped behind her, authoritatively inspecting her plate.

She closed her eyes, feeling the warmth of his presence looming over her. And she smelled his cologne – that all too familiar scent that before she hadn't paid much attention to. Now, it had her high. Floating. Remembering...

Remembering all the times she'd laid against his chest – a chest so broad, it needed its own zip code. She recalled all the time they spent together. Laughing. Enjoying each other's company. She was starting to feel for him more than what she wanted to feel. More than he probably wanted her to feel. There was nothing more confusing, more mind-boggling, more *agonizing* than trying to determine whether or not you were worthy of someone else's love, especially when that *someone* was only supposed to be a friend.

Deciding that the food was okay for her to eat, Royal picked up her glass of orange juice and the carton, then walked toward the sink. He dumped out the glass of juice first, then he poured the entire contents of the carton down the drain.

"What are you doing?" Gemma asked heatedly.

He didn't answer. Instead, he refilled her glass with ice and water. He walked back to the island, set the glass next to her plate and took the barstool next to her. Not across from her, but next to her, sitting in a way that afforded him a good side view of her face while his knees touched her left thigh. "There. That's better."

Gemma looked at him, narrowed her eyes and grew even more irate when he met her obvious irritation with a closed mouth smile. "Why'd you do that?" she asked.

"I told you I didn't want you drinking orange juice."

"Okay. You're not my doctor or my daddy."

"Nor do I claim to be. And since you're already mad at me, what do I care if you get mad over some orange juice?"

She held his stern gaze for a few moments before she turned away from him, determined not to let him get under her skin but it was a little too late for that. She stirred around rice in her plate, feeling legitimately confused right now. Why was he here tonight, anyway? He was already coming by tomorrow to take her to the doctor, so what made him show up early? And why was he just sitting there staring at her, his eyes boring into the side of her face? He wasn't saying a word. Just staring.

Gianna took a fork full of rice and a little meat to her mouth.

Royal watched her chew then stole a piece of broccoli off of her plate and tossed it into his mouth.

"Why are you so mad at me, Gemma?" he asked, chewing.

With a closed mouth, she released a long breath through her nose. Steaming. "You *did* just pour out my drink."

"Don't give me that. This has nothing to do with orange juice. You were already mad at me and quite honestly, *I* should be the one who's upset," Royal said. "After all, you *did* hang up on me last night after I specifically asked you not to."

"I didn't hang up on you," she snapped.

"You did," he said evenly, his temper more controlled than hers.

"You said goodnight to me, did you not?" she asked him. "I said goodnight back to you and that was the end of that."

"You hung up on me," he said, raising his tone.

"So what?" she said, matching his tone. "I didn't want to talk to you anymore and quite honestly, I don't want to talk to you now."

"So what?" he said back.

"Sooo, leave me alone," Gemma told him.

"Umm...I think not," Royal said. He took another piece of broccoli from her plate and tossed it into his mouth. "Why are you mad at me, Gemma?"

Gemma chewed slowly, still annoyed – her appetite fading away with the constant stares of Royal.

"Is it the Paris thing? Is that it?"

She glanced over at him again, her heart fluttering just off of his good looks alone. She hadn't seen him at all yesterday and apparently, he hadn't shaved. His beard was growing in thick and she loved the look of it – made her fingers ache to feel it. Today, however, she wanted to choke him rather than play with his facial hair.

He raised two dark brows. "Is that it?" he asked since she still hadn't answered his question.

Gemma dropped her fork on her plate and took a sip of water. She'd rather have orange juice, but...

"Okay, since the cat got your tongue, I'll just make assumptions.," Royal said. "What would make you think I wouldn't come by and say goodbye to you before I left for Paris, Gemma? You act like I'm leaving tomorrow."

"I don't care when you're leaving. Just leave me alone, Royal."

"I'll leave you alone when I'm ready to leave you alone."

Her glare was as sharp as broken glass when she looked at him and said, "Yeah, because that's your thing, right? Entertain me until you get bored, then it's on to the next woman to keep you on your toes because you're done with the sick girl."

To Royal, her unwarranted words actually stung like a bullet to his heart. Suddenly the man who never let words bother him knew what it felt like for words to actually stab him deep within his soul. And they hurt because they came from *her*.

"And you know what else, Royal?" she asked, pushing her plate away. "I don't need you checking up on me. I don't need you telling me what to eat or drink. I don't need *you*, period, so leave me alone."

Royal frowned. "You're talking to me this way?"

Gemma stood up. "I don't see nobody else in here." She walked away from the table, heading out of the kitchen.

"Everything alright in there?" Ramsey asked from the dining room.

Their voices must've carried there. Royal hadn't realized how out of control the conversation-turned-argument with Gemma had gotten. In the heat of the moment, things had gotten out of control. "Everything's fine, Ram," he said, hot on Gemma's trail.

She was halfway up the stairs when he began jogging to catch up to her. He grabbed the doorknob to her bedroom at the same time she had. With his body cradling hers and his hand on top of hers, they opened the door together as if it was a two-person job. He wrapped his arms around her wiggly body from behind and lifted her up just high enough so her feet weren't touching the floor, stepping into the room, then closing the door behind them.

"Put me down right now," she demanded.

He lowered her to her feet and caged her right there up against the door. "This is how you talk to me, now?" he asked. He was so much taller than her, he only saw the top of her scarf when he looked down at her. "Look at me," he told her.

"Move, Royal."

"Look...at...me," he requested more firmly.

She did as he asked, tilting her head upward to meet his dark gaze.

Still frowning, he asked, "This is how you talk to me now?" searching her eyes for answers. And when he felt her hands push against his torso, he secured her wrists and extended her arms above her head. He was upset but still, he had enough compassion and self-control not to hurt her.

"Stop," she said, staring deep into his dark eyes, completely at his mercy.

"This is how you talk to me now? After everything we've been through?" he asked, his chest rising and falling in and out in rapid succession.

"Let go of me, Royal," she told him. With his body pinned to hers, she could barely move despite her efforts to wiggle out of his hold.

"No," he said, trying to connect his eyes to hers again, but she'd turned away from his intense, angry gaze. "Look at me," he said.

With misty eyes, she connected her gaze to his again, but where was Royal? This guy, the one who was breathing heavily and looking at her with fire in his eyes certainly couldn't have been her friend Royal. *This* guy looked like he could devour her. "Royal, let go of me," she said nervously.

He leaned down, so close to her face that their noses Eskimo kissed. He released her arms, then used his hands to cradle that beautiful face of hers like he was holding something delicate. He *was* holding something delicate. That's how much she meant to him.

Using his right thumb, he traced her lips and kept his gaze locked on her eyes as if this was his first time ever seeing her. He felt her lips quiver beneath the pad of his thumb and saw the confusion on her face as he touched her this way. Confused because she thought they were just friends. She couldn't see that he wanted more, but she would see and feel it now.

He pried her mouth open using that same exploratory thumb when he said, "I will never let you go, Gemma." Then he slipped his tongue inside of her mouth, feeling her body lock up as he did so. He couldn't wait any longer. His taste buds had been watering for the taste of her for the longest, so he took the plunge deep inside of her mouth. He wanted to kiss her so badly, the kiss turned into a feast by the way he was going in, pulling her tongue into his mouth and savoring it greedily with long, powerful strokes – letting her feel the full power of what a man's tongue was capable of. He licked and stroked every part of her mouth that his tongue could reach, determined to kiss her into oblivion.

He knew he was on the right path when he felt her cave in and loosen up to his aggression. Her arms closed around him easily as she pulled him in closer – so close that he could feel the tremors running through her body at the intensity of the kiss. Relentlessly, he rolled his tongue inside of her mouth, alternating with gentle biting on her baby-soft lips. And he pushed his body closer to hers while his hands stroked her waist, causing her body to jerk even more. And then those hands traveled to that apple bottom he loved, squeezing, while his tongue stayed lost in her mouth. Rolling and tasting.

"Mmm," he growled, angling his head from side-to-side, making the penetration deeper as he savored the flavor of love in the recesses of her mouth. He nibbled her lip again, and groaned, hungry for more of this like five straight minutes of kissing hadn't been much of an appetizer to appease his ferocious hunger for her. Lost in the moment, he slid his hands underneath her shirt and touched her smooth bare back.

"Mmmm..." she moaned. She wanted to

expel a breath, but she couldn't do that with their mouths fastened together. "Mmmm," she moaned again her hands trembling against his back. Her moans became louder. Heartbeats more rapid. He squeezed her in his thick arms harder, steadily rolling his tongue. Sucking her lips. His hands migrated to her bottom again and he squeezed. He instinctively pressed his body to hers over and over again for a twofold purpose – making her feel the firm bulge behind his zipper and using his body to keep her stable since feeling her knees buckle.

Gemma couldn't believe this was happening even in the process of it happening, but after she got over the shock of it happening – of them kissing – she enjoyed every intoxicating pull of his sweet, sensual lips. Her moans turned into whimpers. Long, elongated, drugging whimpers – sounds she hadn't known she was capable of making. She also hadn't known that a man could take control of her body. He released her mouth, watching her gasp uncontrollably while trying to force herself to stop moaning but to no avail. And her body was shaking. Her breathing – heavy and wild – as she experienced something she'd never experienced in her life but watched enough romance movies to know exactly what was happening to her body to give her contractions and spasms and cause her to nearly lose consciousness. But how could this happen from a kiss alone? Were his lips *that* powerful? Or was it because it was *him* and deep down, she'd wanted him all along?

"Are you still mad at me?" he asked her.

The deep tone of his voice seemed to prolong the aftershocks of her pleasure. Just looking at him was doing something to her – down there.

"No," she gasped, her body steadily trembling. Her face was completely flushed.

"Do you still want me to leave you alone, Gemma?" he asked, his voice laced with confidence like he knew her answer would be in his favor.

She could hardly catch her breath. Heaving, she responded, "No."

Royal leaned closer and left a soft kiss on her freckled covered cheek. Then he pressed his lips to hers. Grabbing her butt, he effortlessly scooped her up into his arms.

Gemma wrapped her legs around his waist and her arms around his neck as their mouths fused together yet again. She could feel him walking backward to the bed until he sat down, still holding her, still kissing her – more like making love to her mouth. Making sensations strike her all over again from all angles.

He released her to study her. To see the love on her face. But he also saw the confusion, too.

"Why did that happen?" she asked. Her lips were still tender, as well as her breasts for some reason, and her head was spinning. The sensitive area between her thighs pulsating.

"Why did what happen?"

"This. Why did you kiss me?"

"Because I wanted to," he told her. He wasn't trying to sound cocky although that's how it came across. He was just answering her question. "Why did you kiss me back?"

"Um...because I—I think I wanted to, too," she answered, then shyly looked away from his gaze.

He smiled, satisfied. "Look at me," he told her.

She looked at him. Smiled. "Why do you want me to look at you?"

"So you can get used to *us*. We're *not* going back to *just friends*, Gemma. Not after this. I need you to be okay with that. That's why I need you to look at me. You need to know beyond a shadow of a doubt that I want this. That I want *you*. Do you understand?"

She nodded.

"Open your mouth and acknowledge what I'm saying."

She glanced at his mouth when she said, "I'm kinda nervous to open my mouth with it being this close to yours but yes, I understand."

"Good," he said, taking her lips again. Sucking them. Teasing them. "Mmm," he moaned. "You're just as good as I imagined you would be."

Gemma looked surprised. He'd imagined this?

"I would like to spend the night with you, Gemma."

Her eyebrows raised while her hands gripped his shoulders. "Here? In my bedroom?"

"Yes. Here. In your room. In your bed. Just me and you."

"O-okay."

"First, though, I want you to finish your dinner. Can we have dinner together?"

Gemma smiled. Although she didn't think she could stomach any more food tonight, she replied, "Yes."

"In that case, you know you're going to have to turn me loose so I can get up, right?" he asked her.

"Why? You carried me over here, didn't you?" she told him, then moved her legs so she could stand to her feet again. Her legs were still weak, but stable. "I feel like I need to change my underwear before we go back downstairs."

"No. Let them stay on so it can serve as a reminder of what I did to you."

"Royal!"

He grinned. "Come on. Let's go," he said, clutching her hand.

Hand in hand, they went back downstairs to the kitchen, observing that Gianna and Ramsey were still in the dining room.

"Oh," Carson said, looking up at Gemma. "I tossed out your plate, madam. I didn't think you would be returning. Shall I make you another?"

"Yes. With just a little rice, Carson."

"What about for you, Sir?" he asked, looking at Royal.

"Sure. Give me some of everything you got. It smells good. I wanted to get some when I first came in, but I had some business to take care of first." He winked at Gemma.

She blushed with already reddened cheeks and thoroughly kissed lips. This time, Royal sat across the island from her, probably so he could stare and reminisce about what just happened between the two of them.

When Carson was back with plates, Royal immediately started eating, looking up across the table at the woman he loved. Kissing her was more satisfying, more gratifying, more filling than his best meal. And it was more meaningful and enjoyable than with any other woman. He couldn't wait to have her all to himself again tonight.

"Let's discuss a few things," he said.

"Let's," she said, still high from their kiss and at the realization that Royal *was* really into her like Gianna and Carson had suspected.

"Did you really think I would leave the country without saying bye to you?"

"It wasn't that I didn't think you wouldn't say bye. It was the fact that I—I didn't want you to leave me. I still don't."

Royal's chewing slowed. "I don't want to leave you either, baby, but I have to do my job."

"I know."

"And another thing...I know we joke around a lot but I need to make something very clear to you. I don't care how mad you are at me or how upset I am with you—please, please, please, please do not *ever* hang up on me."

"I'm sorry. It was rude of me and it won't happen again."

His eyes crinkled, pleased with her apology. "Okay. Now, on to more important matters...did you get a package today?"

Gemma snorted a laugh and covered her

mouth. That's what he meant by *important matters*? "Yes, I got the pillow, silly. I didn't think you were actually going to buy it."

"I told you I was. That's one thing you'll learn about me. I'm a man of my word."

"And a good kisser."

He smiled big. "Speaking of kissing, I thought you told me you've never kissed anyone? Never been touched. All lies, weren't they?"

"No. I haven't been touched," Gemma said, tickled. "Why do you think I'm lying?"

"Because you nearly kissed me right out of my boxers."

Gemma chuckled. "What else was I supposed to do? You had me pinned upside the door."

Royal laughed. "I just want to know where you learned to kiss like that."

"Movies."

Royal quirked up his lips. "I'm not buying it."

"I promise. Remember in *Think Like A Man* when Michael Ealy was trying to woo Taraji. And that kiss on the balcony...it's like permanently engrained in my mind. Michael Ealy is such a good kisser."

Royal lifted a brow.

"But not better than you, of course."

"Nice save," he told her.

"Is everything alright in here?" Ramsey asked, stepping into the kitchen.

Gianna was right beside him, alert and focused on Gemma.

"Yeah, man. Everything's fine," Royal told him.

Gemma smiled at the inquisitive look on Gianna's face.

"Sure about that?" Gianna asked.

"Yes. Everything's fine, sis."

"Oh, by the way, Gianna," Royal said. "Don't be alarmed, but I'm staying with Gemma tonight."

"Um...why?" Gianna asked.

"Since I'm taking her to the hospital first thing in the morning, I figured I may as well. Either of you have any objections to that?"

"No," Gianna said.

Ramsey looked at Gianna sideways. "Did you say *no*?"

"I did." Gianna smiled.

"You don't have anything to say about Royal spending the night?" Ramsey asked, just for verification.

Gemma covered her face, embarrassed.

"No," Gianna replied again. Normally, she would have said something, like restricting Royal to one of the guest bedrooms or making sure there was no hanky panky going on, but she said nothing. She already knew how Royal felt for her sister. She didn't need anyone to spell it out for her. Even if Gemma couldn't see it yet, she could.

"Okay, then. You two enjoy your dinner," Ramsey said.

"Goodnight," Gianna told them because once she went up to the third floor, she wasn't coming back down.

"Goodnight Gianna, and Gianna Jr.," Gemma said, looking at Gianna's stomach. She was showing a little now going into her fourth month of pregnancy.

"Goodnight guys," Ramsey said, then clutched Gianna's hand and led her out of the room.

Chapter 16

After dinner, Gemma retreated to her quarters to shower and prepare for bed. Royal went to get his overnight bag and suit out of the car because even though he was spending the night and taking her to the doctor, he'd still planned on going to the office afterward.

Bummer, she thought. She could get used to having him all to herself. That got her to thinking well into the future – what if this thing with Royal went beyond boyfriend and girlfriend? What if friends became lovers and lovers, in turn, became husband and wife? *Husband and wife?* She grinned to herself. *No way.* Royal never talked about marriage in any context. Is marriage something he looked forward to, or did he have objections to it? Did men his age think about marriage? Most men didn't regardless of their age, so why would he?

"Gosh, we really need to talk," she mumbled to herself as she shut off the shower. "Or am I being all Gianna-*ish*? Should I just go with the flow and be quiet about this? See where this thing takes us?"

After she dried off, she slid into a pajama set – a sherbet orange tank top and short shorts.

He'd seen her in it before, but something about exposing the length of her legs to him now made a shiver run up her spine, probably because he would try to grab them the first chance he got with his affectionate self.

"Hey," he said as soon as he saw her emerge from the bathroom.

"Hey," she responded, instantly feeling goosebumps flutter over her whole body. She tried to dismiss the feeling by casually walking over to the nightstand to grab the bottle of lotion that she left there. She picked it up, flicked the lid to open it and at the same time, she glanced up at him, watching him pull his shirt up over his head. The nerves in her hand jolted, and the bottle slipped from her grasp. When it hit the floor, lotion splattered everywhere. "Oh, shoot."

"What's wrong?"

She bent over to pick up the bottle and he came walking around the bed to see what she was doing. "I dropped it."

"You dropped it? Just like that?"

"Yeah. It just slipped out of my hand."

Royal walked to the bathroom to grab some paper towels, and when he came back, he kneeled to wipe up the spill while saying, "I've never known you to have butterfingers. You must've been distracted...checking me out again, huh?"

She giggled. "I was." She sat on the bed's edge.

"You should've just told me you wanted some lotion on that sweet body of yours. I can handle it."

"No, I got it."

"I got it all over my hands now...may as well put it to good use," he said, crawling closer to the bed while on his knees.

"Royal...stop it."

He gripped her calf muscles and said, "Shh...lay back. I got this." His eyes swept over her body. "All of this."

"Royal..."

"What's wrong? You don't want me to touch you?" he asked, while purposely massaging already.

"No, I like it. I just think we need to be doing more talking than touching right now. This *thing* between us, whatever this is..."

"You're my girl. That's what this is." He leaned forward and pressed his lips to her right knee.

She smiled. "I've never been anyone's girl."

"Well, lucky for you, now you're mine." Royal rubbed lotion between his hands to warm it, then lowered them down to her skin creating gentle pressure on her thighs. And then he manually pried her legs open wider so they were on either side of his torso and he was in between, still on his knees, massaging. He used his thumb to work the inner thighs, kneading and rubbing the soft skin on up to the juncture of her thighs.

Gemma's lips quivered. "Oh, Lord, help me."

He chuckled. Were her eyes really rolling back in her head? He knew he was capable of bringing a woman maximum pleasure but just the pure act of kissing and massaging seemed to be doing it for her. "You act like I've never touched you before."

"You have, but not my biscuit."

His eyebrows raised. "Your biscuit?"

"Yes."

He chuckled. He had an idea of what she referred to as her *biscuit,* but he wanted further clarification just for kicks. "What's your biscuit?"

"That," she said pointing to the area between her thighs.

He laughed. "That's a new one. Why do you call it a biscuit?"

She shrugged. "That's what Gianna calls it."

Figures. "A biscuit, huh?" he asked, still laughing.

"Yep."

"Well, in that case, I need to go see if Carson can find me some grape jelly to go along with it."

Gemma squirmed, closing her legs tight, but he pried them back open again and said, "Okay, I won't touch the biscuit—at least not tonight."

"Royal!"

"What? You act like it's not going to happen. At some point or another, that biscuit is going to get bitten."

"Royal!"

He was so busy laughing, he couldn't apply the lotion properly. "Alright, let me focus. I'm about to get you all lathered up baby. Lay back."

"No. I told you I got it."

"I'm not gon' mess with your biscuit, Gemma. Just lay back."

"Okay," she said and laid back on the bed.

Royal did a full once over of her body, then started with her legs, listening as she moaned softly at his touch. And then, he rubbed and massaged her toes, one by one, digging the pad of his thumbs into the arch of her feet.

Gemma wiggled. She never knew it would feel this good to be touched by a man. And when he told her to turn over on her stomach, he straddled her, mindful of his weight and massaged her back in heated strokes feeling her quiver beneath his hands. When he was done, he placed the bottle on her nightstand and laid on the bed, opening his arms to her.

She crawled over to him and happily drowned into his calming embrace.

"I think Gianna knows something is up between us," he told her.

"Why do you think that?"

"Because she didn't have any objections with me staying with you tonight. She was cool with it—the same woman who is super protective over you—and suddenly she has no qualms with me spending the night."

"That's because she trusts you, and she knows I trust you, too."

"You do?"

"Stop playing, Royal," she said brushing her fingers across his beard. "You know I trust you."

He pressed his lips to her cheek. "Did you take your medicine already?"

"Yes. I took my medicine," she drawled out.

"Good. You said we need to do more talking than touching."

"That's right."

"What do want to talk about?"

"Us."

"Elaborate, baby. What about us?"

"I'm going to preface this by saying...um...I've never been in a relationship before, so I don't know what questions to ask or not ask...I just know that some things need to be said."

"So, say them," he told her.

"I can't have children."

"Okay."

"That's all you have to say to that?" she asked him.

"Yeah," he said. "What more is there to say?"

She sat up and looked at him. "There's plenty to say, Royal, especially if you want children."

"Gemma, you haven't been my girl for twenty-four hours yet and you're already talking about children?"

"Aren't couples supposed to discuss things like this?"

"Yes, but—"

"Then that's what I'm doing. I'm putting it out there because I don't want you to find out later on down the road when you want babies and I can't have them. That'll be a problem, wouldn't it?"

"Dang, you move fast, don't you, girl?" he asked. He knew she wasn't one to panic, but now, that's exactly what she was doing. He found it endearing because even though the conversation was a bit premature, he understood why she wanted to bring it up so soon. She was thinking long-term about him and his feelings. She was putting herself in his shoes.

"Okay, calm your pretty little self down for a minute," he told her.

"But, Royal—"

"Shh," he said, placing his index finger on her lips.

She opened her mouth and caught his finger between her teeth.

A smile grew on his face. "Alright," he said in a warning tone. "Don't bite off more than you can chew, baby."

"You're not listening to me," she managed to say without releasing his finger.

He pulled his hand away from her mouth and said, "I *am* listening. I heard everything you said. Will you allow me to respond to it?"

"Yes. Please."

"I don't want children," he admitted.

She frowned. "You don't?"

"No. I'm just fine with being Uncle Royal to my brothers' future children."

"Hmm..." she said, thinking it over. "Interesting."

"What's that?"

"I was just thinking...what kind of man doesn't want children?"

He chuckled. "You're kidding me, right?"

"No. I thought most men wanted children to

carry on the family name and all that."

"Sweetie, I promise you I'm being truthful. I never wanted children. You can ask Rom, Ram, Regal or my parents. Take your pick."

"What about marriage?"

He chuckled. "I must've really put that kiss on you, huh?" he chuckled. "Got you in here talking about kids and marriage. What's next, Gemma? A big house on the lake with white picket fences? A dog? You want to know where I see myself in five years? Ten?"

Gemma smiled and returned to her position of lying on his chest. "I'm sorry. I guess I'm just anxious for this to work now that I know you like me."

"It will work. I'm in this for the long haul. I don't want anything about us being short term. And to answer your question, yes, I *would* like to get married one day. What about you?"

"Ummm...I'm not sure."

"What do you mean you're not sure?"

I never thought about it in detail. "It's one of those things in life that I didn't think was possible for me."

"Well, now it is."

She smiled softly against his chest. *Yes, it is.*

Chapter 17

"Gemma, baby," Royal said softly. He'd gotten up early to take a shower and dressed – all so he could watch her sleep for a while. His hands ached to touch her but he couldn't. He didn't want to wake her up. She already had to get up early for this appointment. He wanted her to get all the sleep she could get.

But now, at 7:55 a.m., it was time for her to wake up. The appointment was 10:15 a.m. in Charlotte. With the headache of morning rush hour traffic and having to take the convoluted mess people around here referred to as I-77, they needed to leave between 8:30 and 9:00 in order to get there in time.

His eyes settled on her soft, pink lips – they appeared as soft and delicate as those beauty marks sprinkled on her face. She'd been through so much. It felt good to see her happy for a change. To know she would have a future. With him.

"Gemma," he whispered again, and this time, he leaned closer to touch his lips to hers, breathing in her essence. She was lucky he willed himself to take things slow with her although the intimate kiss they shared yesterday around dinner had gotten out of hand. Some things just couldn't be helped, especially when you knew you were with the person you loved. "Gemma, sweetheart, it's time to get up."

"Go away, Royal," she said drowsily, pulling the sheet up over her head.

"No. You have an appointment today, remember?"

"Nooo."

"Yes."

"My goodness...why do they have to make these appointments so freakin' early? Next time I'm making my appointment for four o'clock in the afternoon." She stretched.

Royal pulled the sheet down so he could see her face, then said, "I don't think they make appointments that late. Now, come on, Gem. We gotta get going, bae."

Gemma pulled the sheet up over her head again.

He smiled. "Okay...what do I need to do to help you get ready?"

"Take my pajamas off and carry me to the shower."

"Oh. You should've said that first," he said, tugging at the waistband of her shorts.

She giggled, slapping his hand away. "I'm kidding, Royal. Get those big hands away from me."

"You weren't saying that yesterday."

She blushed. "Your tongue was halfway down my throat. How was I supposed to say anything?"

"Right," he said.

She grumbled with displeasure at the thought of getting out of bed. "Okay, I'm getting up." She sat up, yawned again, then rubbed her eyes and looked at him. "You look good by the way. You always look so doggone good in your suits. Have I ever told you that before?"

"Maybe, but it's nice to know you've been thinking it all this time."

"I have. I was just too embarrassed to say it." She stood up and stretched her arms up in the air so high, her top rose up, exposing her belly button.

Royal snuck a peep. "Why?"

"Because I thought it was out of line for me to be commenting on how good you looked when we weren't together.

"Come over here," he requested.

She walked over to the bed until she was standing in front of him.

"Now, that you're mine," he said, grazing his fingertips across her mid-section, watching her body jerk in response to his touch. "You can complement the heck out of me."

"Ugh...you men," she said, running her fingers across his rugged beard. "Always want your egos massaged."

"I want more than that massaged," he said, grabbing her backside again.

"Alrighty...that's my cue to take a shower. I'll be right back," she said, quickly walking away from him.

"Don't be too long. We gotta hit the road."

"Okay."

* * *

Going to the doctor wasn't one of Gemma's favorite things to do. It always served as a reminder that she was sick – well not *sick* anymore but still in the midst of her battle. The possibility of something going wrong was always at the back of her mind. And now she had more reason to worry.

Sitting on the patient bed in the room while waiting for the doctor to return, she glanced up at Royal. He was sitting in a chair, looking at his phone – doing work-related stuff she imagined – while they waited for the doctor to return. Now that she had him and he'd made it clear that she was *his* woman (she smiled thinking about that) she had so much to live for. Before, she only had her sister, and while their sisterly bond meant everything to her, it wasn't the same as having the attention of a finer than life St. Claire man. All the feelings she used to brush off and keep to herself were now bubbling to the surface with the realization of their new relationship. Royal was smooth in every sense of the word. Even his caramel skin looked creamy and delicious, and she'd always liked the bearded look on him – wild or tamed. It didn't matter. He was fine enough to pull anything off. And he always dressed sharp especially when he went to work. Royal was the complete package and had a sensuality about him that she was just learning to appreciate.

He looked up, caught her gaze and a smile automatically came to his face. "Daydreaming about me again?" he asked.

She darted her tongue out at him.

He placed the phone in the inner pocket of his suit jacket and stood up. "Is that an invitation?"

"Don't come over here trying to kiss me, Royal," she said failing to hold in a giggle.

"Why not?" he said, stopping immediately in front of her, crowding all of her personal space.

"Because the doctor is going to be back any minute, now go sit down," she said, nudging his chest.

"Nope. Shouldn't have stuck your tongue out at me, now give it here."

She smiled. "Royal..."

"Give it here," he said again, lowering his mouth. When she tried to protest once more, he took the liberty of taking what he'd been after – a literal mouthful of her, kissing her like he was satisfying a craving. Even after he heard the knock at the door, he shamelessly kept on kissing her.

"Ahem," the doctor said. "I can come back if you need me to," he joked.

Royal tore his mouth away from hers until the sound of their lips parting made a smacking noise. "You're good, doc. Gemma was begging me to kiss her and I couldn't resist."

Amused, Gemma said, "You better stop your lying."

"Don't try to play shy in front of the doctor,"

Royal said.

"Okay, lovebirds," the doctor teased. "Your X-ray looks good, Gemma. I sent refills of your medication to the pharmacy and I would also like for you to start on Echinacea to help keep your immune system nice and strong."

"And this is just the over-the-counter supplement. Is that correct?" Royal asked, taking Gemma's hand into his as he looked at the doctor.

"Yes. Over-the-counter."

"Is there a particular brand you recommend?"

"No. They're all one in the same. If you want to go with a name brand, it's up to you."

"Okay."

"And that's it. I'll see you again in a month, Gemma."

"Wait. Before you go, I have a few questions, doc," Royal said.

"Yes, Sir."

"What about sex? Is that okay for Gemma?"

Gemma's mouth fell open. She could just wring his neck. Was he...? Did he...? Why was she even surprised?

"Well, as you know, this sort of diagnosis does cause a lot of fatigue and even the medications can cause nausea. With those factors, a person is not necessarily thinking about sex, but sex is not out of the question. I guess it would just depend on how Gemma's feeling. And, too, there have been cases of vaginal dryness, but of course there are ways to combat that."

"Okay," Royal said squeezing Gemma's hand. "I just want to make sure I'm not hurting her in any way because sometimes, my sweetheart doesn't tell me things."

But we haven't been physically intimate, Gemma thought, although Royal was giving the doctor a different impression.

The doctor nodded. "That's understandable but you should be okay."

"Good."

"Alright," the doctor said. "I'll let you get dressed and then you can check out at the front."

"Okay. Thank you," Gemma told him.

As soon as the doctor closed the door, Gemma stood up, slipped into her jeans while still wearing the paper gown and asked, "Why'd you ask him that, Royal? We're not even having sex. We just started this relationship and you're already trying to get in my pants."

"Trying," he said, amused. "If I wanted to be in your pants, I'd be in them."

"Ugh...stop being arrogant with me."

"I'm not trying to be. You leave me no choice, girl. I wasn't asking him about that because I wanted to take you back to my place and have my way with you. I mean, I do, but not right now. I want the time to be right, and when it is, I want the assurance that I'm not hurting you while trying to make love to you. That's all."

"Okay, got it. Turn around so I can put my bra on, please."

"Do I have to?"

She grinned. "Yes. Turn around."

Once he did so, she quickly put on her bra before he could sneak a peep then hurried up and slipped into her shirt. "You're going to work now, right?"

"Well, I have to take you back home first."

"Actually, I arranged for Carson to pick me up."

Royal frowned. "Why?"

"Because I didn't want you to drive all the way back to Lake Norman just to drop me off, then turn around and drive all the way back to Charlotte to work."

"It's not a big deal for me to drive you home. Call Carson and tell him to go."

"No, Royal. That doesn't make any sense. I can just ride home with Carson and you can go on to work."

"Alright," Royal said somberly, doing a horrible job of trying to hide his frustration. "Ride home with Carson."

"Royal, it's nothing to get upset over."

It *was* something to get upset over when every moment, every minute, every second of the day he had to spend with her mattered to him. But, pushing his feelings aside, he opened the door. They stepped out into the hallway and were on the way to checkout when he said, "I'm not upset. I had planned on spending that time with you today, too. That's all. I try to make the most of the time we have together, especially since you're living in Lake Norman and my life is here in Charlotte. My condo is here. My job. Everything is here except you."

Gemma inhaled deeply and proceeded to the checkout desk understanding exactly what he was saying in not so many words. Her being in Lake Norman was a problem for him. He wanted her with him or perhaps closer. But how?

After she finished checking out, as well as arranging her appointment for next month, they walked outside where Gemma saw Carson's Lincoln parked in the fire lane. He was already waiting for her and Carson must've seen her, too, because he was pulling up to them now.

"So, I guess this is goodbye," Royal said.

"Stop it, Royal. You act like you'll never see me again."

"I won't today. After work, I have to get home," he said as his hands conformed to the shape of her head. He angled her head up so she was looking at him. "I'm really starting not to like this."

"What?"

"Us leaving each other," he said. "It doesn't feel right anymore, or is that just the way *I* feel and you're perfectly okay with it?"

"I don't like it either."

"Then I think we need to talk some things through."

"Agreed," she said.

"I'll call you tonight."

"Okay, and by the way, Royal...no one knows we've been sneaking around kissing and stuff. Gianna may suspect something, but...um...no one knows I'm your girl just yet."

He looked slightly amused. "Are you telling me this because you want me to make an announcement?"

"No. I'm telling you this because you're staring at me like you're going to kiss me right in front of Carson."

He smiled. "Carson knows how I feel about you. I call the man every day to check on you. And even if he doesn't know, now he will," he said, pressing his firm, hot lips to hers and when he settled his hands at the nape of her neck, he proceeded to slip his tongue inside of her mouth and devour her right there. Didn't matter who was watching. He had to satisfy his taste for her here and now.

Gemma was certain she would've floated away if he wasn't holding her. Her pulse quickened as she massaged her tongue with his and tried to handle the mouthful that he was giving her. As they neared the kiss, he used those powerful lips to suck on her lips again, then leave smaller kisses around her mouth.

He released her and said, "I'll talk to you later. Don't forget to pick up your medication on the way home."

"I won't."

He opened the passenger door and spoke briefly to Carson as Gemma got inside. When she was comfortable, he maneuvered his tall body to lean inside and put her seatbelt on before giving her a kiss on the cheek. "Take care of my girl, Carson."

Carson smiled. "I will, Sir."

With that assurance, he closed the door,

then watched Carson slowly drive away.

Carson looked at Gemma, staring at the big smile on her face.

She could feel him staring at her so she looked over at him and asked, "What?" She couldn't stop smiling.

"Am I to assume Royal still gets on your nerves, madam?"

Blushing, she replied, "Sometimes. Yes."

The old man grinned and said, "Sure he does," before turning onto the street.

Chapter 18

As soon as Royal arrived at the office, he sat down, opened his laptop and checked his emails. One that caught his attention right away was an email from Ramsey:

From: Ramsey St. Claire
To: Royal St. Claire
CC: Ralph Sheppard; Gilbert Lewis
Subject: FW: ! Lumber Issue w/UC Project

Royal,

See email from Ralph below. Need this handled before your Paris trip.

Thanks,

RSC

---------- Forwarded message ----------
From: Ralph Sheppard
To: Ramsey St. Claire
Subject: Lumber Issue w/UC Project

Ramsey,

Trying to be proactive here instead of reactive. There will be a lumber shortage for the University City Project if we don't go ahead and get a backup supplier lined up. I've checked out some possible alternatives if you would like to pull a meeting together with Royal to discuss.

Thanks,

R. Sheppard
Project Manager

Royal immediately dialed Ralph's extension.

"What's up, Royal?"

"Hey, Ralph, how's it going, man?"

Ralph sighed. "This UC project is going to be the death of me."

"Yeah, I was just reading an email that Ramsey forwarded to me about a lumber problem. What's going on with that?"

"Okay, so there is a shortage for the type of lumber we're using for this site. I knew this could be an issue if we went with a higher grade of lumber instead of the standard, and sure enough, we have a problem."

"Yep. I remember when you brought up the issue in the early planning phase. That's why I already have two suppliers on standby with reserves set aside for us—Genesis Suppliers and K.B. Builders. All you have to do is submit a request through purchasing and they'll handle placing the order."

"Oh," Ralph said. "Are they already set up in our system?"

"They are."

"Well, crisis averted. Which company do you

recommend I contact first?"

"Go with Genesis. They should have enough to hold us over."

"Awesome. Thanks, Royal."

"Not a problem. Listen, if you have any other issues, feel free to come to me with them. Don't bother Ramsey unless you absolutely have to. I was hired to tackle these kinds of problems."

"Okay. Will do, Royal. Thanks again, man."

"Yep," Royal said, hanging up. After he did so, he immediately replied to Ramsey's email that all was well.

"Yo!" Regal said, barging into Royal's office.

Royal glanced up at him. "What's up, Regal?"

"Nothing much. Just stopped by to see if you were ready to do this Paris thing."

"Nah...I would be just fine staying here."

Regal's brows went up. "Are you sure about that? I thought you'd be glad to get away from St. Claire Architects for a while. Seems you and Ramsey always got beef."

"Man, Ramsey is just being Ramsey. I know how he is. I don't even think he can help it."

"Okay, then forget all that. Why are you not interested in Paris? And why weren't you at the status meeting this morning?"

Royal focused his gaze on his brother. "What's with all the questions, Regal? You sound like the auditors."

Regal chuckled.

"If you must know, I wasn't at the status meeting because I didn't get in today until noon," Royal said as he typed another email. "I had to take Gemma to the doctor."

"Oh. Gemma. You've been spending a lot of time with Gemma lately."

Royal glanced up at his brother and continued typing. "Yeah. I have."

"Why?"

Royal smirked. "Because I like being with her." He didn't owe his brother an explanation, but he figured he'd give him an honest answer, hoping it would be enough to send him on his way. He had work to catch up on and he couldn't do that with the inquisitive stares of his brother. He looked up at him again. He wondered why Regal looked surprised. His brothers – all of them – knew that Gemma had been stealing his time as of late. Shoot, even the last time the brothers had hung out, Royal wasn't there. He'd opted to be with Gemma instead.

"I know you like being with her," Regal commented. "You've ditched us several times for her."

And I'll ditch you every time for her. Royal loved his brothers, his family, but there was something about loving Gemma that couldn't compare to any other kind of love he'd ever felt in his heart. He smiled. *Isn't that how a man knew when he'd found the one?* "She's special to me, Regal."

"Ah...*special*," Regal said rubbing his chin. "Sounds like you're going to be looking for rings in Paris, bruh."

"That's already on the agenda."

"What!" Regal nearly jumped out of his

chair. "Stop playing with me, Royal."

Royal couldn't fight the smile that came to his face. "I'm not playing. I love Gemma."

"You what!" Regal was beside himself – completely floored with Royal's confession, so much so that he slapped his own darn self to make sure he wasn't imagining this. "You're serious."

"I am."

"And Gemma knows how you feel?"

"I haven't told her that I love her yet, but I'm sure she already knows."

Regal shook his head in disbelief. "And you're not pulling a fast one on me?"

"Nah, man. I wouldn't joke about this."

"Who else knows about you and Gem?"

"I talked to Ramsey about it—"

"And he didn't give me the heads up," Regal said since he and Ramsey usually discussed everything. "I see how it is."

Royal offered a bemused smile. "Do you, Regal?"

"Yeah. First, Ramsey marries *little miss cupcake* and now you're claiming the sister. So, y'all got loyalties now, huh? The two married brothers versus the two single brothers."

Royal leaned back in his chair and chuckled. "Slow your role. I'm not married yet."

"Yeah, but from what I gather, it won't be long."

"Look, Regal. I love her. End of discussion."

"I don't think so. Mother called a dinner this Sunday since she got word of us leaving for Paris on Monday. If you bring Gemma, and I'm sure you will since you can't *stand to be without her*, mom's gonna pick up on it right away. You know you can't hide anything from her. Not a thing."

"Then that's something I'll have to deal with, but Gemma's definitely coming with me."

"Well, if you don't want mom peeping you two out, do yourself a favor."

"What's that?"

"Stop staring at Gemma like she's a fresh piece of hot-out-the-grease chicken."

"But she's finger-lickin' good."

Regal stood up and said, "Alright. I'm outta here."

Royal chuckled as Regal exited his office.

Chapter 19

Gemma had showered and was waiting for a call from Royal. She wasn't killing time by watching a movie or tidying up her room. She was sitting on the bed staring at her phone, waiting for the thing to ring. She glanced at the clock: **9:47 p.m**. Why hadn't he called yet?

She grabbed her emoji pillow and squeezed it close to her chest. Maybe he was tired and went to bed early. No, this was Royal. He didn't get tired. He had the stamina of a rodeo bull and that was without any caffeine boosters and energy drinks. So, where was he? When she couldn't handle waiting any longer, she picked up her phone to dial his number and her phone buzzed in her hand. It was him. A smile instantly came to her face.

"Hey," she answered.

"Hey. You must've been on your phone already, huh?"

"No. I had just picked it up when I saw you calling."

"Oh. How are you, Gemma?"

"I'm good. How are you, Royal?"

He chuckled. "Why do we sound so formal? I'm supposed to be like, *wassup bae*. And then you're supposed to follow up with, *whattup handsome*."

She giggled. "I like how you automatically assume I'd call you handsome."

"You wouldn't?"

"Well, yeah, I would."

"Okay, then. Quit playing with me." He chuckled. "Anyway, how was your day after we parted ways?"

"Good."

"Carson wasn't trying to drill you for information was he?"

"No. Not at all. Plus, you took my tongue so I couldn't talk, anyway."

"Funny," he said.

"Oh, and I picked up my meds on the way home and took a nap once I got here, of course."

"What about dinner? What'd you eat?"

"Soup. Carson made some vegetable soup just for me."

"Cool. I'll have to thank him when I see him."

"How was your day at the office?"

"It was work. I had a few fires to put out...nothing your boy couldn't handle."

She smirked.

"Hey, I found out from Regal that mother is hosting dinner at her house this Sunday since she knows me and Regal will be out of town. I would like for you to come with me."

"Are you sure?"

"Yes, I'm sure," Royal said.

"But—but we haven't really told anyone

about us yet."

Correction: you haven't told anyone. "We don't have to actually tell anyone anything, Gemma. People can come to their own conclusions."

"So, you're okay with your parents knowing about us?"

"I am, but I want to focus on us being us before making my parents aware of us."

"In that case, I shouldn't go."

"Why do you say that, bae?"

"Because you St. Claire men like to stare at your women. You stare at me a lot, just like Ramsey stares at Gianna. And your mother is going to peep that right away."

"What if she does? I don't care."

"I do. Your mom's nice, but I can't read her. I don't know if she likes me or not."

"Are you kidding? My mother likes everybody, and she thinks you're a doll."

"You think so?"

"I know so. Why would you think otherwise?"

"Because I saw her looking at me all weird because I had the scarf on."

"She probably wonders why you're wearing one."

"What's there to wonder about? She knows I had cancer, right?"

"Yes, but you have hair, Gemma."

She did have hair but not the hair she used to have. Her hair used to be long, thick and curly. Now, it was about four inches long, still curly but lacked that same luster and beauty it once had.

"What are your plans for tomorrow?" he asked.

"What's tomorrow?"

"Friday."

"Oh. Right. I'm going to the bakery with Gianna tomorrow."

"Perfect."

"Why's that perfect?"

"Because I want you to spend the weekend with me and it would be convenient for me to pick you up from the bakery, so pack a bag."

"Um, excuse me?"

He snickered. "There's no need to pretend you don't want this just as much as I do."

Gemma chuckled. "How did I not see how arrogant you were before?"

"It's not arrogance." *More like love. The need for your love. An obsession I have with you.*

"Then what is it, Royal?"

"Spend the weekend with me and maybe you'll find out."

Gemma smiled. "Let me stop giving you a hard time. Of course, I'll spend the weekend with you. I miss you so much I can't stand it. I was sitting here practically tongue-kissing this emoji pillow before you called me."

He laughed. "You just made my night. Pack a bag before you go to bed. I'll pick you up from the bakery as soon as I'm off work."

"Okay, Royal. Have a good night."

"Thanks to you, I will. Sweet dreams, baby."

Chapter 20

Gemma erased the message on the chalkboard and wrote the cupcake of the day: blueberry cream cheese. She also refilled the milk refrigerator after the delivery was dropped off and brewed fresh coffee. She restocked the cups and lids, stirrers and napkins, and after all of that, she watched Gianna as she frosted cupcakes.

"You do it so flawlessly," Gemma commented.

"I try...funny how I make them look so good right before they're devoured."

"Gotta get people's mouths watering somehow, right?"

"Yep, and it's all about presentation, my dear."

"I see."

Gemma leaned up against the counter.

"So, you're staying with Royal again this weekend, huh?"

"How'd you know that?" Gemma asked, crossing her arms.

"You put a bag in the backseat of the car this morning. That's why."

"Oh. Right. My bag." *Busted.*

Gianna stopped frosting, then looked up at Gemma.

"Yes. I'm staying with him this weekend. He's picking me up from here."

"I see. Sounds like you two are getting serious."

"We're...um...we...hmm..."

"You're at a loss for words," Gianna said, "Something that usually never happens to you which means, you're trying very hard to make up a lie or avoid telling me the truth."

"I like Royal a lot."

"Okay, so have you kissed him?"

"Aren't you being intrusive?"

"Nope. You wanted to know every detail of my first date with Ramsey, remember?"

"Yeah, but I wasn't being all judgy with you, Gianna."

"And I'm not being judgy with you. I just want to know where you two are in this supposed *friendship* of yours."

"I like him."

"I know you *like* him, but has like turned into—"

"Don't say it."

Gianna's eyes brightened. "You love him!"

"Gianna—"

"O-M-G...you wuv, wuv, wuv him," Gianna said, doing a dance that looked like a broke down, sad version of 'the twist'.

Gemma couldn't wipe the smile off of her face. "The word is love, not *wuv*, and—"

"So, you're admitting it. You *love* him."

"Okay," Gemma caved. "Yes. I love him."

Gianna screamed like the building was on fire.

"Gianna, stop! You're going to scare the patrons."

"I don't care. My baby sister is in *wuv*," she said, pinching Gemma's cheek. "I'm so happy. Yes! We both love St. Claire men. We can compare notes now. Give each other advice. This is too freakin' awesome."

"Let me give you some advice—zip your lips! Royal doesn't know I *wuv* him and I don't want to scare him off. Men and love don't get along sometimes."

"Girl, please. Why do you think he wants you at his condo all the time?"

"This is only my second time spending the weekend with him, and why do you sound so happy about this? I thought for sure your neck would spin all the way around. Like twice."

"Nope. I'm genuinely happy for you. You're finally going to know what it feels like to be in love. Awesome!"

"Gianna, keep your voice down."

"I can't help it. I'm so excited."

"Yeah but this is Royal we're talking about. He told me he got bored with women easily. Said he was dating this one woman who, to me, sounded like she was perfect. He said she didn't hold his interest. If *she* couldn't hold his interest, how am I supposed to?"

"Girl, I don't think you're going to have a problem with that. You're plenty of complicated to keep Royal on his toes."

"I guess you have a point there," Gemma

muttered. "But he makes me nervous, too."

"In what way?"

"Intimately. He's—"

"Wait...have you two already been intimate?" Gianna asked with her hand over her heart.

"No. I'm just freaking out about the idea of it."

"Oh. Shrew. Well, I was the same way with Ramsey."

"How was it? Is it—painful?"

"Um...no. I'm not gon' lie though—the first time is a little uncomfortable, but then after that, it's—" Gianna nibbled on her lip. "It's pure bliss."

"That's not telling me anything."

"What do you want me to do? Go into detail and describe what goes here and there—"

"No," Gemma interrupted. "I want to know how it made you feel. Like, do you feel closer to Ramsey now after making love to him?"

"I do. When you love someone and you keep that in your head when you're intimate with that person, it'll reinforce that love every single time."

Gemma smiled. That's exactly what she wanted to hear.

* * *

Towards the end of the workday when all the customers had left and it was time to close up shop, Gemma turned off the light for the *Open* sign. That's when she saw Royal's white Tesla pull up. She immediately felt giddy. She hadn't seen him since noon yesterday and now, here he was. She stood there at the window and watched him get out of the car, wearing a suit that was as black as his beard. He looked exceptionally good and she couldn't believe this man was actually hers. Or was he hers?

Her eyes followed his every step toward the bakery. He had on a pair of dark sunglasses, so she couldn't tell if he'd spotted her staring or not. She didn't care if he did. She missed him and couldn't stop staring. She wanted to run out there and jump up into his arms, but the sight of him had her frozen in her tracks.

When he walked into the bakery, she turned to look at him. "Hey."

"Hey, you," Royal said, looking around to see if Gianna was anywhere in sight. He wanted to snatch Gemma up in his arms immediately upon stepping in without the interruption of her sister. He'd seen Gemma through the window, staring at him. It made him quicken his steps to get to her faster. He leaned forward and convinced himself to leave a kiss on her temple instead of taking her mouth, then asked, "Where's your sister?"

"In her office."

"I'ma go speak, then we can ride out."

"Okay."

Royal walked on to the back, saying, "Where you at, woman?" right before he came up to her office.

Gianna looked up, and a smile grew on her face when she caught sight of her brother-in-law. "Well hello there, Royal?"

Royal gave her an inquisitive frown. Why was she looking at him with a sneaky smirk on her face? "You probably already know that I'm taking your precious Gem with me. I just want you to know she's in good hands."

"I know that." She waggled her brows, then glanced at Gemma who'd crept up behind Royal. Gemma was making faces, trying to get Gianna to stop talking.

Royal slid his hands into his pockets and glanced back at Gemma who hurried up and put a smile on her face, then he returned his focus to Gianna. "My flight leaves early Monday morning. I'll see you at dinner on Sunday, right?"

"Yep."

"I'll ride back home with you after dinner, Gianna," Gemma spoke up to say.

"Okay. Sounds good. Now go. Have fun."

"Okay. Bye, sis."

Royal followed Gemma to the front door, took her bag from the floor then opened the door so she could exit ahead of him. He put her bag in the trunk and opened the passenger side door for her like a gentleman.

"Thank you, Royal."

"You're welcome, beautiful."

He walked around the car quickly, slid the key into the ignition, but didn't start the car. He looked over at her instead.

Then, as if his eyes forced her to, she looked over at him, more like at those tasty lips of his. She watched him lick them before he leaned over towards her. Her mouth automatically opened for him, allowing the clearance he needed to slide his tongue inside and do a full sweep of her mouth before taking a longer concentrated, deeper kiss. One that had her fingers trembling around the strap of her purse. One that had soft moans coming from her throat at regular intervals.

He broke off the kiss and looked at her, noticing her eyes were still closed. "Ready?"

She opened her eyes and felt a weird feeling like this was the first time she was actually seeing him – the man she was falling in love with. He was everything and then some. Unbelievable in every way. "Yes. I'm ready."

"Sure? You look like you're lost."

"My head is cloudy right now. That's what your kisses do to me."

He smiled. "But you're okay, right?"

"Yes. I'm fine."

"Okay. Good." Royal started the car, ready to take his baby *home*.

Chapter 21

Once they arrived at his condo, they'd changed clothes and gone for a walk to a restaurant down the street – a different one this time – to grab some dinner and now they were back, chilling on the sofa. He was on one end and she was on the other with pillows behind her head while Royal fiddled with her toes. They were supposed to be watching *Jumping the Broom*, but he was too busy tickling her feet and she was too busy laughing.

"Stop it, Royal. Gosh. I should've never told you were my ticklish spots were."

"I would've found them, eventually."

"How?"

"By exploring your body inch by mouthwatering inch. That's how."

"My body is off limits."

Royal raised a brow. "To who? Not to me."

She smiled. "Yes to you," she said. "I'm new to this dating stuff, but I would like to know that a man is mine and mine only before giving him my body."

"So you want to be married first because if that's the case, that can be arranged," he said.

She giggled, but he wasn't laughing. He had

a straight face, staring at her like he was ready to say vows today had she gave the word. He let go of her feet then crawled up the length of her legs so that his body blanketed hers. He snuck a kiss from her lips then stared down at her in an adoring, endearing way.

"What?" she whispered, looking up into his eyes while her hands lay flat against his back.

"I love you, Gemma."

Seemed her heart stopped, eyes glazed over with wetness at hearing these words from him. The crazy thing about it was, this wasn't the first time he told her that he loved her. But all the other times were casual. There was something distinctively different about this particular time – how intently he was looking at her and how she could feel a part of him firm and pressed against her thigh. But maybe she was getting things twisted. For her own confirmation, she said, "I know you love me, Royal."

"No. I'm not talking about casual, slap-you-on-the-booty-and-you-think-nothing-of-it love. I'm talking about love—the kind that has me thinking about you every second of my day. The kind that makes me want to leave work early to see you. The kind that makes my heart flutter when I see you smile. The kind that has me so turned on right now, all I want to do is make love to you, but I won't because you deserve a man who would be willing to marry you before taking your innocence. Before making you his, and that's what I intend to do. I. Love. You."

She squeezed out a tear, still in disbelief. "I

love you, too, Royal."

He smiled. "More than the slap-booty way?"

She giggled while a small tear of happiness made an appearance. She wasn't a crier but some feelings just couldn't be hidden. "Yes. More than that. I think about you all the time, too. I just never thought you'd be interested in me beyond friends, but these last few days have proven me wrong."

He kissed her tear away, then parted her lips with his, tasting the saltiness of the tear that had escaped. "Am I too heavy for you?" he whispered in her ear before outlining it with his warm, wet tongue.

Gemma shivered. "Yeah. A little."

He immediately got up and stood next to the couch. He didn't want to do anything to hurt her. "Take your meds and meet me in the bedroom."

"I thought we were going to watch this movie," she said, sitting up.

"We were. But that was before I knew you were in love with me. Now, all I want to do is feel you in my arms and play with you a lil' bit."

Tickled, she asked, "Play with me? What does that mean?"

"You'll find out when you get your lil' butt up in here," he said, walking down the hallway. "I'll be waiting."

Gemma walked to the kitchen where she'd unzipped her purse then removed her pill container. She took a bottle of water from the refrigerator and after taking her meds, she pulled in a deep breath and started down the hallway to where she knew she'd find Royal. He was just where he said he'd be—in his bedroom, waiting for her. He'd taken off his shirt and was sitting on the bed in a pair of Polo shorts.

"Come on over here. Don't be scared now."

She crossed her arms, slowly walking towards him.

He knew she was nervous. Who crosses their arms when they walk? The position looked awkward and dangerous. She couldn't see where she was going. What if she tripped over his shoes and injured something? His sweet little thing didn't need any more hospital stays.

"Uncross your arms," he told her. "You look defensive like you're preparing for battle."

"That's the thing...I don't have a clue what I'm walking into right now. Do I need to be prepared for battle?"

Royal moved to the bed's side, sat there and waited for her to close the distance between them. When she was finally standing immediately in front of him, he said, "Straddle me."

She suddenly got a twitch in her right shoulder. Her nerves were getting the best of her.

Seeing her nervousness – the slight layer of sweat on her forehead, dilated pupils in a set of beautiful eyes and stiff posture – he took her hands into his and attempted to calm her down. "Look at me."

"I *am* looking at you."

"Barely. I want you to look into my eyes."

"Stop trying to seduce me, Royal."

He chuckled. "Funny how women nearly beg me to seduce them and you're asking me not to try with you."

"Well, I'm not other women," she said connecting her gaze to his.

"And that's what I love about you. Now, straddle me."

Gemma moved her knees on either side of his taut thighs, then fully straddled him by stretching out her legs until they folded behind his lower back. She circled her arms around his neck. "I'm here," she said. "Now what?"

"I can show you better than I can tell you," he said, darting his head forward to nip at her lips, leaving small kisses around her mouth. Then he looked at her, connected his vision to her darkened honey brown gaze. She smiled, then shied away, nestling her face in the curve of his neck.

"Oh, Royal," she said in a voice a little higher than a whisper.

"Talk to me, baby."

"I just find this so hard to believe—" she began with her lips brushing against his neck. Then she adjusted to an upright position so she could look at him. "We were friends, now we're *this* and I just never thought..."

"Never thought what?"

"That anyone would love me. That's why I spent so much time watching romance movies. I never knew love and romance were possible for me, that's why I enjoyed watching other people finding it—even if it was fictional."

"Well, you no longer have to wonder, sweetie, because you have me," he said, cupping her backside. "And I've grown to love you more and more every day. And you know what?"

"What?" she asked, staring into his eyes and then her eyes, filled with twinkles, roamed every inch of his face.

"I'm glad we started off as friends first. It gave me a chance to know you and fall in love with the person you are on the inside and not just chasing after you for your exquisite beauty."

"Exquisite...you act like I'm a princess or something."

"You are a princess. My beautiful princess." He kissed her again, joining their mouths in a sweet crash of desire. With each pull of her lips, each stroke of his tongue, he wanted more. That's why when he felt how she sucked and latched onto his tongue, fire burned all the way down to his abdomen while his hands held her firmly in place. And they kissed for what seemed like an eternity this way – hot and heated – desire building and building until Gemma broke off the kiss to breathe. She closed her arms tight around Royal's neck and just soaked this all in – him, his love, the fact that he was hers – everything. Her heart pounded with nervousness and anticipation. And she had plenty of reasons for both as she ran them through her mind:

1. Royal had never been in love, so what made

him fall for *her*?

2. She had never been in love, so how did she know it was real?

3. She was still a virgin.

4. Royal definitely wasn't a virgin.

5. She was twenty with no career, no college, no license.

6. Royal was twenty-five with a career, a Bachelor's Degree and comfortable life.

7. She was a lung cancer survivor and in many ways still fighting.

8. He was the perfect picture of health. The only pills he took were vitamins.

"Gemma?"

"Yes?"

"Are you intentionally trying to choke me?"

She loosened her grip on him and laughed. "Sorry. I was just thinking about us. I guess I got a little lost in my thoughts."

"It's okay, Gemma. I'm just teasing you. You can squeeze me as hard as you want." He grazed under her blouse and stroked her back. And then those hands traveled in the opposite direction towards the waistband of her jeans. With little effort, he was able to breach the waistband to touch her softness.

"Mmm," she hummed.

He fell back on the bed so she was lying on top of him. With her legs outstretched now, he had more clearance to cup her cheeks in his hands the way he longed to while she took more control of the kiss – using her tongue to play with his – losing herself and letting go, getting comfortable with him. Exploring.

She pulled her lips away from his and kissed his chin, down to his throat and on down to his Adam's apple. She savored this part of him, licking and flicking her tongue across it.

"Bae?"

"Yes?" she asked, steadily licking.

"You do know that's not a real apple, don't you?"

Gemma dropped her head, cradling it into his neck and giggled. "I'ma bite it anyway if you keep on teasing me."

"I don't mind, baby. You can bite whatever you want. I can handle it."

"I bet you can," she said, rising up on her elbows to look at him, practically in awe. "I still can't believe we've crossed the line."

"We have, and there's no turning back now."

She planted a light kiss right on top of his nipple and whispered, "Yes...no turning back now."

Chapter 22

"You're telling me that this is your first time behind the wheel of a car," Royal asked with disbelief as he sat on the passenger side of his car while Gemma sat in the driver's seat acting like she could barely touch the wheel. It was Saturday morning, and they were in the parking lot right out in front of his condo.

"I've sat behind the wheel of my new Jeep Compass Ramsey bought for me, but I haven't driven it anywhere."

"Other than that...this is the first time you're behind a wheel of a car."

"Yeah," Gemma said, playing with the seat buttons trying to find one for the backrest.

"So, you've *never* driven a car?" Royal asked again.

She stopped what she was doing and looked at him. "No. I know it's hard to believe, but, no, I haven't. It's lame. I get it."

"It's not lame. It's just interesting, but I understand."

"You know what I don't understand," she said, finally finding the right button to adjust the seat.

"What's that?"

"How you're able to drive this car while you're sitting in the trunk?"

He chuckled. "The seat wasn't *that* far back, and you know I have long legs, baby."

Yes, you do. Long, muscular hairy legs. Yummy. She still had her hand on the button, moving the seat forward when she asked, "Okay, so how do you explain the backrest laying on the back*seat.* I couldn't even see over the steering wheel."

"Because you're so petite, Gemma. I'm a lot bigger than you in case you haven't noticed. Now, let me school you. Pay attention. This...is...a...key," he said, holding up the key to his car and talking super slow. "You...stick...the...key...in...the...keyhole. We...call...that...an...ig-ni-tion." He laughed.

"You're not funny, Royal. I know what a freakin' ignition is."

"Here," he said, handing her the keys. "Crank it up, then."

She took the keys from his grasp. She cranked up the car and said, "Whoa, baby! This is neat."

He quirked a smile, feeding off of her excitement. "Okay. Before you get all gas-pedal happy, you need to know about these gears. Anytime you shift a car out of park and into *reverse* or *drive*, you need to press the brakes."

"Okay. Got it."

"Alright, so press the brake."

"Right now?"

"Yes. Right now. You *do* know which one is the brake, don't you?" Royal asked, amused,

"Because if you don't, you may as well get out of my car."

"Yes. I know where the brake is."

"Okay. Press it."

Gemma pressed down on the brake using her left foot.

He smiled. "Also, I should point out that you do not use your left foot when you're driving. You should be using your right foot for everything."

Gemma looked confused. "For the brake and gas pedal?"

"Yes. For the brake and gas pedal."

"So my left foot just sits around and does nothing."

He chuckled. "If that's the way you want to look at it. Yes."

"That just seems like too much work," she said, making the adjustment.

"Well, that's the way it goes, darling. I can guarantee you that you *will not* pass a road test if you're caught with your left foot on the brake pedal."

"Alright, alright. I got it. What do I do next?"

"Are you pressing on the brake?"

"Yes."

"Okay. Move the gear into 'R' for—"

"Reverse. I know that much."

"Yes. Reverse, and don't take your foot off the brake after you do it."

"Alright," she said shifting the car into gear.

"Easy enough, right?" he asked her.

"Yeah. Easy. Now, what do I do?" she asked, taking her foot off of the brake. The car began moving backward a little. "Ha! We're moving," she said, excited. "We're moving!"

"Wait, Gem. Step on the brake."

"Oh, my bad," she said, then attempted to step on the brake but hit the gas pedal instead. The car flew backward.

"Gemma, hit the brake!" Royal yelled. "Hit the—"

Gemma slammed on the brakes so hard, they were now sliding backward, crashing into a light pole. "Oh my God! Call 9-1-1!" Gemma shouted.

He looked at her and couldn't help but laugh even though he knew her nerves were rattled. "We don't need to call 9-1-1. Nobody's hurt. Well, my car is, but—"

"Then what was that we ran into?"

"*We* didn't run into anything," Royal said tickled, shifting the car into park. "*You* backed into a light pole." He got out, surveyed the damage. Sure enough, there was a pretty big dent in the bumper.

Gemma got out, too, then walked to the back to see the dent. She covered her opened mouth with both of her trembling hands. "I can't believe I did that."

"You're shaking. It's okay, Gemma," he said embracing her.

"It's not okay. I wrecked your car."

"Hey, screw the car. Look at me." When she looked up at him, he said, "Forget about the car. I just want to make sure you're okay."

"Yeah. I'm okay," she said, steady trembling. "I just feel bad about—"

"I told you don't worry about the car. Now, why don't you walk over there so I can move it back in the parking space before somebody calls the cops?"

"Okay," she said solemnly and walked toward the sidewalk. But she didn't wait there. She continued on inside of his condo where she sat on the couch and buried her face in her hands, trying to get her nerves together but she was having a difficult time doing so. She couldn't believe she actually drove into a pole. How was she going to get her license like this?

Royal surveyed the damage. There was an indentation where the bumper came into contact with the pole, but that was it. While the damage was minimal, he estimated that it would cost at least five grand to repair. Not a problem for him. But the minor accident had him thinking about the major accident he was involved in five years ago. He downplayed the seriousness of it to Gemma when he'd told her about the scar on his abdomen but that same accident had knocked him into a coma for two days. Had his family on edge, wondering if he would come out of it. Her backing up into a pole instantly had him flashing back to that moment – when he was on the way home one day, glanced in the rearview mirror and saw the car sliding straight for him, coming too fast for him to react or attempt to duck out of the way. All he could do was brace for impact. Two days later, he woke up in a hospital bed.

Maybe that's part of what drove him to Gemma. There was something about watching her recover – watching her fight to live, if for nothing else, for her sister. He'd had a similar fight and now, a bump into a light pole was enough to remind him of how precious life really was.

He walked inside still not giving two cents about his car. He found Gemma lying in the center of his bed. He crawled over the bed until he was lying in front of her. Her eyes opened.

"Hey. You okay?" he asked.

"Yeah...just tired now."

He knew that meant she was still upset, but nonetheless, she needed her rest. "Okay. You know I'm cool about the car, right?"

She cracked a smile.

"I am, Gem. As long as you're okay, I'm okay."

She touched the side of his face and watched his eyes close. "I'm okay. I just need to rest for a while. That's all."

"Okay." He pressed his lips to her forehead and said, "Rest and don't be in a hurry to wake up. I'll have dinner ready for you later."

"Okay. Thank you, Royal."

Chapter 23

While Gemma slept, Royal ordered takeout – a creamy cheddar broccoli soup with a side of shrimp scampi. He figured it would be just enough for her and since he frequented the restaurant, he knew the food quality was up to his standards. Therefore, she would like it.

He was on the living room floor doing pushups when he heard her say, "Working off your frustrations, huh?"

He stopped, looked up at her and said, "The only frustration I have to work off is having to leave for Paris." He stood up, embraced her warmly.

"I see you shaved your beard down some," she said, staring at his face, touching his hair.

"Yeah, just a little. If I went one more day without shaving it, you wouldn't be able to see my eyes."

She laughed. "It wasn't that thick."

"Oh, yes it was," he said. "Did you sleep good?"

"I did."

"Hope you're hungry," he said, leaning forward to press his lips to hers. "I ran out and got us some dinner."

"Good. I'm starving."

"Then come on. Let's eat."

Royal warmed up the food and prepared a bowl for them, then served the shrimp on plates. Before he touched his food, he looked at her to watch her taste the food first, making sure it was to her liking.

"This soup is good. Shrimp is, too," Gemma said.

"I knew you'd like it. Isn't that amazing? I *know* you, Gemma Jacobsen."

"It is." Gemma drank some water, thinking about how nice it would be to have a small glass of orange juice, but Royal would probably have a conniption-fit had she asked for some. "Hey, Royal, can I ask you something?"

"Yes," he said, making sure he gave her his undivided attention.

"Does it bother you that I'm only twenty?"

Royal tossed a shrimp into his mouth. "Why would your age bother me? You're twenty. I'm twenty-five."

"Yeah, but you can drink. I'm underage."

"So what?" He shrugged. "You don't drink, anyway."

"You're missing the point. If I *could* drink, I wouldn't be able to because I'm twenty."

"You don't have to keep saying how old you are, Gem. I'm fine with your age, or is this about you not being comfortable with an older, mature, experienced man?" His eyebrows rose.

"No, it's not that. I just wanted to know what your thoughts were," she said, but it was much deeper than that. Since waking up early and having time to filter through her thoughts after sleeping on it, Gemma compared their current place in life. She'd done it before, tried to dismiss it, but here it was again, staring her in the face. Apparently, their differences really did bother her if it was constantly resurfacing.

"Royal."

"Yes, Gemma?"

"You're so far ahead in life and I'm just starting out. I don't even know how to drive a freakin' car."

A quick frown disturbed his features. "I told you it wasn't a big deal to me."

Gemma closed her eyes and rubbed them. "But it's a big deal to me," she confessed. "Royal, I'm having a hard time trying to see how I fit into your world as a girlfriend. As a friend, I didn't have this problem. As your *girlfriend*, I feel inadequate and I don't like that feeling. I don't want to feel like Julia Roberts in *Pretty Woman*—like I'm not good enough for the wealthy, handsome businessman."

Amusement lightened his features. "Didn't she play a hoe in that movie?"

"A prostitute, yes."

"So, you're comparing yourself to a prostitute?"

"No, Royal. You're missing the point I'm trying to make. I never thought I would get to this stage in life of actually having feelings for someone, but I have them for you. The only thing is, now I'm having feelings of inadequacy—"

"All because of the accident?"

"Not only that. It's also because—I'm—"

"Don't say sick," he told her. He wiped his mouth with a napkin. "Because you're not sick anymore, Gemma."

"Then what am I? I'm still taking pills. Still going to the doctor once a month. Do you know why I'm going once a month, Royal? So the doctor can monitor me and make sure the cancer doesn't return."

"Yes, preventative care. We all get checkups—"

"But you've never had tumors growing inside of your body. You don't know what it feels like to live from one day to the next not knowing if the tumors will come back and you'll have to undergo surgery all over again. You don't know how that feels, Royal."

Royal didn't say a word, but that was his way of absorbing his frustration – internalizing it so he didn't unleash it all on her at once. He just finished eating the few shrimp he had left and finished a bottle of water. Then he sat there and stared at her. She'd since stopped eating and had ceased eyeing him down for a reply. She was just sitting there, looking uncomfortable and out of place. Like she didn't belong.

"You're right, Gemma. I don't know how it feels to have cancer. I do know that you have to live your life and stop being afraid of what's going to happen. You have no control over that. None, whatsoever. How can you live, baby, if you're constantly worried about dying?"

Gemma blew out her cheeks. He wasn't getting it. "So, I'm just supposed to pretend I don't have any concerns."

"No. You're supposed to live your life, and you can start by taking off that scarf."

She frowned. "I'm not taking off my scarf."

"You need to," he said, his gaze sharpening. "You have a scarf in every color to match every outfit you wear, and it's not like you need it. You're just stuck, Gemma. Mentally, you've caged yourself inside of this box, waiting for the cancer to come back."

"That's not true."

"Then prove me wrong."

"I don't have to prove anything to you."

The muscle along his jawline was so tight, it's a wonder he was able to flash the haughty grin that came to his cheek. "That's where you're wrong. Take off the scarf, Gemma."

"No. And for your information, I wear the scarf because I don't like my hair. My hair used to be long and pretty. Now, it's short and ugly."

"It's not ugly. Take off the scarf."

"No."

He steepled his fingers while seconds of silence passed between them, giving her time to think it through. To conform to his request. "Gemma, if you don't take it off, I will."

"You're threatening me now?"

"No. I'm not threatening you. I would never threaten you. I'm challenging you. I know you're not used to that, but here we are. You need to remove the scarf. Otherwise, you're proving my point."

"What point?"

"That you're not living...you're still hiding behind your illness. Now, you're telling me you feel inadequate like you have to downgrade and get a man who's *down* to your level since you feel like you're not where I am in life which is ridiculous in itself."

"Ridiculous to you. It makes perfect sense to me." Gemma stood up and picked up her plate.

"I'll get your plate," Royal told her. "Your hands need to remain free so you can remove that scarf."

Just let it go. Jeez. She rolled her eyes, agitated, lowering the plate to the table and turned to walk away. That's when she felt his arm fold around her. All it took was one of them to stop her in her tracks. "What are you doing, Royal?"

"You mad at me?"

"No, I'm not mad," she said resting her hands on his arm. "I'm a little frustrated that you don't understand me."

"I do understand you," he said, manually turning her around so she was looking at him now. "I understand you in ways you don't even understand yourself." He backed her up toward the counter. "Let me tell you what I know about you, Gemma. You're beautiful, and it's not just the outside I'm attracted to. It's everything you are. Everything. But you're still hiding...still afraid to live...afraid to love because of what you think *might* happen. You can't live your life like that, Gem, and I won't let you." He reached for her scarf and she cringed.

"Royal, please don't."

"Trust me. Let go of your fears and trust me." Royal reached for the knot where the scar was secured.

She quivered and grasped his arm with her hand. "No," she said, faintly.

He stopped, looked at her and asked, "Do you trust me?"

"You know I trust you, Royal."

"Then let me." Reaching for the scarf again, he gently pulled it so it came apart. And then he unraveled it and placed it on the counter.

Gemma swallowed hard. The last time he'd seen her hair was when she was hospitalized. Then, he wasn't her man. He was just a friend. What would he think of her hair now? She closed her eyes. If only she had the power to make herself invisible. He wasn't saying a word. She could only feel his fingers strum back and forth across her head like he was giving her a scalp massage. And he took his time, threading his hands through her honey brown strands, enjoying the feeling of its curly texture against his fingertips, acquainting himself with this part of her that she'd intentionally kept from him. He smiled. He loved the texture of her hair. The thickness of it.

"Open your eyes, Gemma."

"No," she said, defiant.

"Come on, baby. Open your eyes for me."

When she finally did, his heart slammed right up against his chest. Her hair and eye color were virtually the same, but seeing the two at the same time did something to illuminate her eyes and brighten her face. He was truly seeing her for the first time.

"And yes, I still think you're beautiful," he said. "And I'm still very much in love with you. I'll always love you, Gemma, come what may, so there's no need for you to be alarmed. No need for you to be scared to love me." He touched his mouth to hers and said, "I'm not going anywhere," and then he then slipped his tongue between her parted lips and indulged in a wet, deep kiss that left her moaning – had her sucking and stroking his tongue with as much need as he was stroking hers.

With her breasts squished to his chest, she felt a new sensation coursing through them – through her entire body. And while he kissed her, his hands squeezed and toyed with certain parts of her body.

Gemma wrapped her arms around his neck and continued her efforts to keep up with him – to match him. To give him the same passion he was dealing out to her, but goodness she was no match for his precision. Didn't matter how many romance movies she'd watched. Royal leaked passion out of his pores, and when a man loved a woman, what could stop him from showing this much passion and desire?

"I think we should take this to the bedroom," he told her as he stared at her lips.

"But I thought you said—"

"I know what I said, and you said you trusted me, correct?"

"I do trust you, Royal," she said, staring

helplessly into his eyes. Her cheeks turned an even darker shade of red when he took her hand and led her down the hallway to his bedroom. The moment they stepped inside, he released her hand. Standing behind her, he raised her shirt up. Without protest, she extended her arms up in the air and allowed him to finish the job of removing it. After he did so, she lowered her arms, feeling exposed even though she still had on a bra. Like he hadn't seen her in a bra before...

He had in the early days of their getting to know each other. He'd helped her get dressed and as far as she was concerned, he was fulfilling the role of Harriet, her former caretaker. Now, she felt tingly all over, trying to pretend she was comfortable but was anything but. When he lowered his mouth to the bridge of her shoulder, her whole body jerked as if he'd ran an ice cube down her back. But just like one adjusts to cold and heat, she adjusted to him by loosening up and letting herself go – allowing herself to feel what he was offering to her. Love.

Royal pulled in a deep breath when he rested his chin on top of her head, inhaling the scent of her shampoo that made it smell so good. Then he worked his way to the other shoulder, moving her bra strap so it dangled around her arm. And now, he had clearance to massage the area with his tongue while listening to her gasp with each flick. Just when she was getting into it and relaxed, his fingertips danced down her flat stomach.

Her whole body jerked. "Will I ever get used to your touch?"

"No," he said while brushing his lips at the nape of her neck. "Do you like my touch?"

"Yes, Royal."

"Good," he said, looping his thumbs at the waistband of her pants and tugging them down easily, revealing her in a pair of silk panties, blue ones, same color as her bra. And while he was pulling her pants down, he went down with them, kissing the back of her thighs on a pair of already weakened legs. He kissed his way to her calves, then when her pants settled around her ankles, he lifted her feet from the floor, one at a time and finished taking them off. Running his fingers along the length of her legs, he stood up again, stepping in front of her this time. He pulled his shirt up over his head. His muscles flexed automatically as he connected his gaze to hers.

She swallowed hard, felt the blood pumping fiercely through her veins as she studied her man's body. His tattoo. *Be true.*

She nibbled on her lip. He *was* the truth. The *whole* truth and nothing but the truth. Her eyes took in the shape of his broad shoulders and the definition of his chest, sprinkled with hair that begged to be touched. Then she studied the outline of his lower V-lined abs. He was more man than she could handle.

"Touch me, Gemma."

"Huh?"

"You heard what I said. Touch me."

"Touch you where?"

"Anywhere you want."

"Um...hmm..." Gemma said thinking of where she thought a man like to be touched. She reached for his zipper and he moved away from her.

"What are you doing?"

"I'm touching you."

"There?" he asked amused. "Of all the places you could touch me, you go for my zipper."

"You said anywhere."

"Yeah, but you don't want to wake up the boss, baby."

"The boss?" Gemma chuckled. "That's what you call it?"

"Yeah."

"From the looks of it, *the boss* is already woke."

"If you think that's woke, then you're in for the shock of a lifetime, bae."

Gemma chuckled some more. Then, laying her hands flat against his pectorals, she asked, "So, can I touch you here?"

"Yes. That's more on your level."

"So squeezing that tight butt of yours is out of the question?'

He gnawed on his lip but didn't answer her. So Gemma took it upon herself to undo the clasp of his jeans, pulling them down.

"Can you step out of those?" she requested.

He did what she asked, stepped out of them, then stared down at his woman with all the love his eyes could gleam. He lifted her from the floor then lowered her to the bed, hovering over her. He dipped his head, kissing her neck, suckling and nipping at it. And then he connected their mouths again, indulging in the succulence that was her lips while his hands explored her body. He touched her breast-filled bra, and she nearly hyperventilated. And then he explored her below, feeling the warm dampness of her treasure and listening while she moaned. And she did something that surprised him. She grabbed a handful of his muscular rear end. The sensation made him deepen his kisses but also made him pause shortly after doing so to take a breath and get a handle on his desires.

"Ah, Gemma," he said before burying his face in her neck.

"What's wrong?" she asked.

"I need to get up."

"Why?"

"Because if I don't, I'm going to—"

"You're going to what?" She grinned. "Surely lil' ol' me don't have mighty Royal at a loss for words."

"I'm going to ravish you." He breathed harder. "You have no idea how much I want you."

"You have me."

He looked at her. "I mean want you as in how much I need to be inside of you. Making love to you. Making us one. Making you mine." Royal sat up and got up from the bed, too hot to be cooled off by anything but making love to her, but not yet. He had to take a step back.

"Royal, don't leave."

"I have to," he said, uncompromisingly,

"And you better be glad it's not raining."

She grinned. "Are you serious?"

He put his shirt back on and said, "Yeah, I'm serious. I'll be back when you're sleeping, and yes, I will stare at you and steal so many kisses, you'll end up dreaming about me."

He kissed her lips, then said, "Goodnight, baby."

"Goodnight."

"I love you."

"I love you, too." She smiled staring up into the brilliance of his eyes. She wasn't sure how ready she was, but one thing she was sure of was how she felt with him. Loved. Special and cared for. Somehow, she knew a life with Royal would be one of fulfillment and joy.

Chapter 24

The family had all settled around the dinner table and after Mason prayed over the food, Romulus said, "You went all out, huh, Ma."

She'd made some barbecue baked chicken, buttermilk fried chicken, potato salad, mashed potatoes, creamed corn and biscuits.

"Yes. It all looks scrumptious, Bernadette," Siderra said.

Bernadette smiled. "Thank you." Compliments about her food were always music to her ears.

"I'm going to be at least five pounds heavier when I leave here," Siderra added.

"Me, too," Gianna chimed in. "That's the fun thing about being pregnant. I can always use the baby as an excuse to eat an extra plate."

Bernadette chuckled. "Yes, you can. I want my grandbaby nice and healthy."

"Yes, indeed, so eat up," Mason added.

As the family dived into their food, smaller one-on-one conversations around the table ensued.

[Ramsey and Gianna]

"I didn't even know I liked creamed corn before this evening. This is delicious," Gianna said to Ramsey.

"Yeah, just like your cupcakes," he told her.

"And this barbecue chicken is the best I've ever had. I really need to spend more time with your mama in the kitchen."

"She'll enjoy that. She's always talking about getting to know you better and cooking just may be the thing that bonds you two—well, at least until the baby arrives. Then you're bonded for life."

Gianna smiled.

Ramsey glanced across the table at Gemma and Royal. Gemma was all smiles, and it seemed Royal couldn't stay out of her ear. "Hey, by the way, how has it been going with Gemma helping you out around the bakery?"

It was Gianna's turn to glance up at Gemma. She looked happy, smiling at something Royal had just whispered to her. She thought her sister looked pretty nice with her curly hair out, not hidden behind a scarf. She even wore earrings today. "She's doing good but I feel like I'm *forcing* her to learn the ins and outs of baking. I don't think it's what she wants to do."

"Probably not. Knowing Gem, she's doing it because she knows you need the help."

"Exactly."

Ramsey wiped his mouth, took a sip of wine, then said, "And since such is the case, we're going to need to go back to our original plan and hire some help. There's no way around it now."

"I know. You're right. It just has to be somebody trustworthy with a good background."

"We'll discuss it in more detail later. I don't want to interrupt your love affair with that corn."

Gianna playfully slapped him on the arm while he chuckled.

[Regal and Mason]

"Son, seems you're in Paris so much, you may as well have a permanent residence over there."

Regal grinned. "Nah. It's cool to visit and do business, but North Carolina is my home. Now, if I go over there and meet a nice, French voluptuous woman, y'all might not see ya boy no more."

Mason laughed at his son. "I don't foresee that being a problem."

"Why not, pops?"

"Tell me the last time you've seen a voluptuous *French* woman."

"Uh..."

"Exactly. What you need to do is stick around here and get you one of these cornbread-fed North Carolina women."

Bernadette caught a part of their discussion and could only shake her head. The rest she wouldn't hear since she was too busy staring at Royal and Gemma.

"I ain't got time to be out here looking for no women, pops," Regal said.

"You don't have to look for them, son. Women are a little more aggressive than they used to be back in my day. They come looking for you now."

Regal shook his head. "Those are the ones I avoid. I'm the pursuer. Not the pursued."

"What about Gianna's friend? The one you kept calling *WB* for some reason at Ramsey's party?"

"Oh." Regal chuckled. "She's a looker, but she got this whole anti-men, Ms. Independent thing going on. Ain't nobody got time for no scorned females with baggage."

"You can say that again," Mason said.

[Romulus and Siderra]

"I really, really like this family," Siderra said. She glanced around the table at everyone.

"They like you too," Romulus told her.

Siderra finished chewing, then asked, "Do you know what I was thinking about before you picked me up tonight?"

"No, but I'm sure you're going to tell me."

She glanced at him, watching him bite a huge chunk of chicken. "I was thinking about how you are my only *in* when it comes to the St. Claires."

"Meaning what, Derra?" he asked right before he sunk his teeth into another piece of chicken.

"Meaning that if I get a boyfriend, I'm going to be—you know—getting to know *his* family. Likewise, when you become involved with someone, you're going to be getting to know *her* family and she'll be sitting here instead of me, getting to know *your* family."

He grabbed a napkin and wiped his mouth. "Why are you even thinking about that?" Romulus turned up a glass of Mountain Dew, taking a big gulp of it.

"It was just on my mind. That's all."

"Then get it off of your mind. You already know I don't do girlfriends."

"Yeah, but—"

"So, why are you bringing it up, unless you've been thinking about getting a man, which I know ain't the case?"

"What if it is the case?" she asked, then tasted the potato salad.

He looked at her, frowned slightly and shrugged casually. "Then we'll cross that bridge when we get to it," he told her. He wasn't about to get in his feelings off of something that hadn't happened yet. The thought of her having a boyfriend had crossed his mind before and made him play through the logistics of their friendship, but he never took it seriously since Siderra was one of those business-focused women. The creative type. She had her own little store where she made handmade items – pillows, blankets, curtains – all sorts of trendy home décor. And the business was such a success, she had other local artisans display their items in her store, to which she received a commission off of every sale. And with hours from nine in the morning to seven in the evening, when would she have time to date?

[Royal and Gemma]

Royal looked around the table. Several times, he'd caught his mother's gaze and smiled at her. They were situated on opposite ends but her constant stares made it seem like she was right there beside him. "Seems like everyone is having a good time," he said to Gemma.

"Yeah. I'm glad we all got together before you and Regal left. I still don't want you to go, though."

"My mother doesn't either. Don't know why she's so protective over me more than with my other brothers."

"Duh, Royal. It's because you're the youngest. You're her *wittle* baby."

"There's nothing *little* about me, girl. You should know that by now."

"Can't argue with you there," Gemma said laughing. After taking a sip of water, she said, "I really wish you wouldn't go, though."

"Why?"

"You know why," she said nudging his thigh.

He leaned close to her ear and whispered, "Because you love me."

She looked at him, quickly glancing at his lips before making eye contact. "Yes."

Still breathing in her ear, he said, "You don't know how much I want your lips in my mouth right now."

"Royal, stop it," she said, blushing.

"Pretend you have to go to the bathroom," he told her. "I'll find an excuse to get up then

I'll meet you down the hallway and shove my tongue inside of your mouth. I need to hear you moan as badly as I need to taste you." He looked at her face and saw it reddening before his eyes.

"Royal, stop," she said breathily with her pulse quickening. "You're drawing attention to us."

He shrugged a shoulder. "So. The bottom line is, you're mine. I should be able to do whatever I want to you whenever I want to do it."

"But you're making me nervous."

He was still staring at her when he said, "Am I?"

"Yes."

"You're going to wish I was here staring at you when I'm thousands of miles away next week."

She connected her gaze to his and said, "Yes. That's true."

He saw the worry in her eyes. "But I'll be back soon enough. For now, just enjoy this time with me and my family, okay, beautiful?"

She smiled. "Okay."

To Royal, it seemed like the entire room lit up when she smiled. It automatically made him smile and move his hand over to cup her thigh. And she placed her hand on top of his and threaded their fingers together underneath the table.

* * *

Bernadette stood up.

"Where are you going, dear?" Mason asked.

"Oh. I have to turn off the oven and take out those pecan pies."

Mason stood up, too, and said, "Let me get the vanilla ice cream out of the deep freezer." He left the dining room along with her.

"Now's a good time for me to make a run to the bathroom," Gemma told Royal.

"I'll come with you."

"No, you won't. Stay here."

"But I want lips."

Gemma grinned. "Royal, I'll be right back."

He sighed evenly. "A'ight, but don't stay too long or I'll be coming to look for you," he said, looking her up and down as she stood up and subsequently walked away.

Gemma made the bathroom visit a quick one as she promised Royal she would. She gave herself a good, long appreciative look while she was still in the bathroom, threading her hands through her curly hair, thinking that it wasn't as bad as she thought it was. Now, all those weeks of hiding it seemed silly. The short curly hair suited her and best of all, Royal loved it.

She stepped out of the bathroom and was coming down the hallway toward the kitchen when she heard Bernadette say, "I'm telling you, dear, Royal's in love with Gemma. Have you noticed how he's been staring at her all night? They're sitting beside each other and he still stares at her. And they were just whispering and laughing it up."

Mason grinned. "So what. They like each

other. She's a good woman. A beautiful woman."

"I agree with you. She is a beautiful woman."

"Then what's the big deal about them seeing each other *if* that's what's happening? We don't even know for certain."

"I'll tell you what the big deal is. We've already had to suffer the pain of watching one of our sons lose someone he loved to cancer. I do not want to go through that again, let alone put my youngest through it."

"Dear, we agreed that we have to let our boys live their own lives. Did we not?"

"Yes, but why let them go through heartache when we can spare them, Mason?"

"Do you really think Royal is not aware of Gemma's condition and what he's signing up for *if* they are dating?"

"Of course he is. He was in the hospital with her for goodness sakes."

"Then let the boy—I'm sorry, *man*—live his life, honey."

"And then what?" she asked with a broken voice. "We're going to allow our son to fall in love with a woman who's sick? Our same son who was diagnosed with depression in high school and who almost died in a car accident five years ago?"

"And each time he came out stronger than he was before. Each and every time. Our sons are strong. Strong minded and strong-willed. As their parents, we need to trust their decisions."

Bernadette sighed, not wanting to admit that

her husband was right.

"Listen, sweetie. I know how much you love our boys. I love 'em, too. But we have to let them live their lives. If Royal loves Gemma, who are we to stop him? We can't tell our children who to love. The only thing we can do is hope they bring a good woman home to us and by all accounts, Gemma's a good woman. Okay?"

Bernadette released a heavy-hearted sigh. "Okay."

GEMMA WAS SO distraught by what she'd overheard, she walked back to the bathroom and eased the door closed behind her. She leaned against the sink and tried not to give into tears. Surely Royal would know something was up if she had. So, she got herself together as best as she could and came out of the bathroom again, returning to the dining room. She noticed Bernadette and Mason had made their way back to the dining room table.

She sat next to Royal.

"I started to come looking for you," he whispered to her.

"It didn't take me long, did it?" she asked, plastering a smile on her face.

"It did. Are you okay?" he asked, examining her further, noticing something with her demeanor was different.

"Yeah. I'm okay. I just feel tired all of a sudden."

"Should we go?"

"No. We can stay. I'm fine." She took a sip of water while feeling Royal's eyes analyzing her.

Chapter 25

Very early the next morning – like 4:00 a.m. early – Royal attempted to wake up Gemma to say goodbye. He'd spent the night with her, at Ramsey's place, since it was more convenient to pick up Regal and roll out to the airport. He spent most the night observing her. She had said she was tired at dinner and almost immediately when they returned last night, she passed out. In fact, even now, she was sleeping so good, he didn't want to wake her but he had to see those eyes one more time before leaving.

"Gemma, wake up, baby."

She slowly moved, stretched and then opened her eyes to see him. "Hey. Are you about to leave?"

"Yeah. I'm going to pick up Regal and then we're rolling out."

"Okay." She reached for him, wrapped her arms around his torso and squeezed.

"Oh, baby, I'm going to miss you, too," he said. "Take care of yourself while I'm gone."

"I will."

"Make sure you take your medicine every night."

"I promise."

"And you can call me, text me...whatever. I don't care what time of day it is." He touched her cheek, then nudged her chin up. "You hear me?"

"Yes."

"I love you, Gemma."

"I love you, too, Royal." She squeezed him again. "Be safe."

"I will."

When Royal left the room, Gemma sat on the bed replaying Bernadette and Mason's conversation. When she was at their home, standing in the hallway, it all felt surreal like she wasn't sure if she was hearing things or not. But she heard Bernadette loud and clear – she didn't want Royal getting mixed up with a woman who had cancer. With a woman who had a greater risk of *dying* prematurely. The bottom line – she didn't want her son with *her*. As harsh as it sounded, Bernadette had a point. Those were the very same concerns Gemma harbored concerning a relationship with Royal. What if she got sick again? She didn't want to put him through that. But she loved him, and maybe that was selfish, but she couldn't help it. Couldn't stop herself from needing his love. Still, in the back of her mind, she also knew that there was some other woman out there who would be better for him. Someone who was perfectly healthy. Someone more on his level in life. Someone his mother would be satisfied with.

Chapter 26

The rest of her day pretty much sucked. Gemma thought about Royal and his parents – this dilemma that kept her questioning herself and her worth. Was she doomed to a life of loneliness after her diagnosis and if she was, how was that any different from dying? Now that she had a good outlook on life, she wanted normality – to fall in love and have a home, a career and start her life. Right now, she was stuck living with Gianna and Ramsey. She didn't have a home. A career. A life. She didn't have anything but Royal and his mother didn't want her to have him.

She sighed, placed a bowl of soup on her nightstand, unable to eat. Maybe she was over-thinking everything and driving herself crazy in the process. She was only twenty years old. Who said her happily ever after had to happen right this instant? What was wrong with taking her time and getting to know herself – her *adult* self – then creating new experiences? Learning from her mistakes. Discovering other people outside of the bubble of people she knew. And she could meet other men, possibly, although no man could ever compare to Royal.

And there was no need to rush into love. She especially didn't want him to since, in her opinion, the only reason he fell for her was because she was sick. They wouldn't have met if Gianna hadn't met Ramsey. If she was any other woman walking down the street with a head scarf, Royal probably wouldn't have said a word to her. There was nothing about her that screamed, *hey, look at me*, with the exception of the scarf and freckles. Otherwise, she was just a plain, ordinary woman.

In addition to the current problems that ailed her, there was unfinished business with her mother. It was different to watch Gianna confront Geraldine but it would be interesting now that it was her turn to talk to her. Did it have to be a confrontation though? Was there any chance the woman could be civil? She wondered...

Gemma picked up her phone noticing the missed call from Royal, followed by a text message:

Royal: We're cruising along and all is well.
Where are you? Call me back.

Deciding her mind was too clouded to call him back because Royal St. Claire would pick up on a problem immediately, she found Geraldine's number and dialed it.

"Hello?"

"Hi, Geraldine," Gemma said, feeling a certain kind of way not being able to call her mother, *mother* or *mom*. She wasn't a mother, so *Geraldine* it was.

"Hi. Who's this?"

"This is... this is Gemma."

"Gemma," she said sounding breathy. "How are you, doll? I haven't seen or heard from you since you left the hospital, I hope all is well."

"I'm doing okay. I was wondering if you could meet me somewhere for lunch tomorrow."

"That would be great. Are you coming alone?"

"Well, I'll be helping Gianna at the bakery tomorrow—"

"Helping? Are you well enough to be doing that messy baking stuff?"

Jeez, don't try to pretend you care. "Yes, I am. I can take a lunch break around noon and we can eat at one of the restaurants out there on the boardwalk if you would like."

"Okay. I'll be there. By the way, does Gianna know about this."

What difference does that make? "No, she doesn't."

"Then it might be best if you met me outside so that maniac husband of hers can't slap me with a restraining order."

Gemma rolled her eyes. *How about he just slap you? That would be more effective than a restraining order.* "Will do. Later." Gemma lowered her phone to the nightstand right before hearing a tap at the door. "Yes?"

"Open up, Gem," she heard Gianna say.

Gemma walked to the door, cracked it open then said, "What's up?"

"What's up with you?"

"Nothing."

"Then why do you look like I caught you doing something."

"Gianna, what do you want?"

"I figured I'd come check on you since you barricaded yourself in the room."

"I'm fine, *smother*. And why are you worried about what I'm doing? Don't you supposed to be with Ramsey somewhere getting fifty shades of greyed?"

Gianna giggled. "Good one, Gemma. Hey, have you heard from Royal?"

"Yes. He sent me a text message and said they were *cruising* along."

"Good. Then I'm going to bed. Are you coming to the bakery with me tomorrow?"

"Yep."

"Cool. I'll see you in the morning, baby girl. Love you."

"Love you, too. Goodnight," Gemma said, closing the door.

Chapter 27

"I'll be back in a lil' bit, Gianna. I'm going to go get some air."

"Okay, sis."

Gemma had already seen Geraldine waiting in the parking lot like an antsy five-year-old and since she didn't want Gianna to know she was going to meet her, she used a quick excuse to leave the bakery for a while. She walked over to Geraldine, feeling a weird sensation of being biologically connected to a stranger. The woman who carried her for nine months and birthed her into the world was the same woman who didn't know her. It shouldn't have been that way, but that's what it was.

"Hey," Gemma said.

"Hey," Geraldine replied and gave a flirty wave displaying her gold rings and long chalk-white fingernails.

"Where would you like to eat?"

"I'm thinking Me-hi-ca-no," she sung, then did a shimmy. "How does Za-pa-ta's sound?"

Gemma shrugged. "Zapata's okay."

They began walking in that direction, neither saying a word. All you could hear was Geraldine's heels pattering on the wooden boards of the boardwalk along with the laughter of children across the way at the small playground near the Hilton Hotel. The awkwardness of the situation threatened Gemma's sanity. She was beginning to wonder if she should have initiated a meeting with her at all. Probably not.

When they were situated in the restaurant, Geraldine asked, "What happened to your hair, child? It used to be so long and pretty."

Gemma's brows furrowed. Why was she asking such a dumb question when she knew about the cancer? "After chemo, I lost my hair. It's growing back, though."

"Hmph...I see why you kept it wrapped up. Why don't you see if you can find a wig or something? All these beauty supply stores around here gotta have something for you."

"Geraldine, I don't need a wig. My hair is fine like—"

"Ooh, we have to get matching margaritas," Geraldine said, cutting Gemma off.

Matching margaritas? What kind of...

Gemma frowned looking up at her. "Do you know how old I am?"

Geraldine looked puzzled for a moment then said, "Old enough for a lil' dranky drank, I'm sure." She cackled, trying to downplay the fact that she didn't know how old her own daughter was.

Gemma internalized her anger. *What a pitiful excuse for a mother.* "I'm twenty."

"Oh. Don't worry about it," she said, waving off the fact that Gemma was underage. "They

229

probably won't card you here."

"It doesn't matter. I don't drink alcohol."

"Oh." She snapped her head back. "Well, whoop-de-doo. Look at you." Her eyebrows rose up in an *oh well* gesture right before the waiter showed up. "Hola, mi amigo," Geraldine said, giving the waiter that same fingery wave. "Give me a mucho, *giganto* strawberry *margarito*—the biggest you got."

The waiter chuckled a bit and said, "Sure, Señora, and what about you?" he asked, looking at Gemma.

"Just water for me. Thanks."

"Okay. I'll be right back with that."

Gemma checked her phone. Royal had tried calling again, followed by another text message:

Royal: where are you?

"So, what is this meeting about?" Geraldine asked.

Gemma tore her attention away from Royal's text message and looked up at Geraldine. Going into this *meeting* with her mother, she wanted to be *un-Gianna-like* and not get in her feelings about being abandoned. But Geraldine was making it difficult for her to keep her sanity.

"What is this meeting *about*?" Gemma repeated.

"Yeah. What's the dealio? Are you trying to get answers about your father, too, just like Gianna? That's why you wanted to have lunch with me, ain't it? Had nothing to do with getting to know your mama. You just want to know who your sperm donor was. Ain't that right, lil' girl?"

"Um...are you mental?" Gemma blurted out before she realized it.

"Excuse me?" Geraldine asked, offended.

"I said, are you mental?"

Geraldine shook her head. "You're just like your smart-mouthed sister...she's turned you against me."

"Leave Gianna out of this, okay. You've blamed enough of your problems on her. I wanted to talk to you because I had my own unanswered questions, and yes, I would like to know who my father is, but first—"

The waiter lowered a glass of water in front of Gemma and a *giganto margarito* on the table in front of Geraldine, along with a basket of chips and a small bowl of salsa. "Are you ready to order?" he asked.

"Give us a minute, amigo man," Geraldine said.

Gemma frowned. She watched Geraldine pick up her glass and drink half of a frozen strawberry margarita without getting the slightest brain freeze. Then again, you had to have a brain to get a brain freeze...

"Why did you leave me?" Gemma asked.

Geraldine did a juvenile eye roll as to say, here we go again and replied, "I already answered this question for Gianna."

"Well, I'm not Gianna. I'm asking for myself. Why?"

After taking a gulp of margarita, Geraldine

said, "I'ma tell you the same thing I told
Gianna. I kept a roof over your head, but I
wasn't one of those *motherly* women. I liked
having my freedom."

"Then if you wanted freedom more than you
wanted children, why didn't you keep your legs
closed?"

Geraldine grew indignant. "I'm not going to
sit here and be *insulted*, Gemma. *You* asked *me*
to come out here, and I obliged. Now, can we
have a decent conversation?"

Gemma sighed. That was her intent initially
– to have a decent discussion but Geraldine
made it so difficult. "So, am I to understand
you left me because you didn't want to be tied
down."

"That's right."

*And you really want to have a decent
conversation with me after admitting that?*
"Give me a name."

"Of who?"

"My father," Gemma snapped.

Geraldine rolled her eyes. Again. "His name
is Logan Spriggs, and do yourself a favor. Don't
contact him. He's living it up in Ballantyne with
his *white* wife."

"He's married..." Gemma said quietly,
talking it through. She looked up at Geraldine
and asked, "Does he know about me?"

"Yep. Sure does. Now, ask me how many
times that buster has asked me about you." She
formed the shape of a zero with her fingers,
then had the nerve to peep through the circle
with her right eye. "If you want to talk to him,

be prepared to be let down."

Gemma shook her head. "I'm used to being *let* down. If a person, a girl, a young woman can't depend on her own mother, I think other disappointments in life will come at a much lesser blow. I guess that's the lesson I learned in all of this. Your failure to be a mother has, in essence, prepared me for all the other letdowns I'm sure to have in life. See, I do have something to thank you for, Geraldine."

Geraldine glared at her daughter for a moment, then plastered a smile on her face before asking, "So, shall we order?"

Gemma's face tightened with anger. The more she interacted with Geraldine, the more she could understand Gianna's frustration with the woman. She had a way of being unbelievably nonchalant after she caused so much pain. Gemma couldn't take anymore. She stood up and said, "On second thought, I'm not hungry. I'm just going to go. Enjoy your lunch."

"Gemma..."

"Have a good day, Geraldine," Gemma said, quickly walking away from the table and exiting the restaurant. She strolled along the boardwalk, heading back to the bakery but taking her time and actually getting that air she told Gianna about. While she walked, she thought about calling Royal back, or at the very least responding to his text messages but since he left, or more like since Bernadette made it clear how she felt about them as a couple, she hadn't bothered. She needed time to think it through, plus she'd watched enough black movies to know that if a man's mother didn't like you, the relationship was destined for failure.

When she stepped back into the bakery, she saw Gianna on the cordless phone. Then Gianna said, "Here she is now. Hold on."

"Hey, it's Royal," Gianna whispered, covering the receiver.

Gemma frowned. *Crap. Royal.* She took the phone then said as upbeat as she could, "Hey Royal."

"Where have you been?"

"I just took a walk."

"I'm not talking about your walk. You haven't been returning my calls, voicemails or text messages.

"I know. I'm sorry. I've just been tired and—"

"Too tired to reply to a text, Gemma?"

"Royal, it's getting busy in here. I gotta go. I'll call you later."

"Gemma—"

"I'll call you later."

"Okay," he said.

"Bye."

"Bye, Gemma."

Gemma sighed heavily when she handed Gianna the phone back.

"You want to tell me what that was about?" Gianna asked.

"What?"

"You told him we were busy and we ain't all *that* busy. Plus, when I told you it was Royal on the phone, you looked annoyed. And why does

234

he even have to call the bakery to get ahold of you? Why aren't you answering his calls?"

"Stop! Enough with all the questions, Gianna. I'm not in the mood."

Gemma took an apron from the rack and tied it on.

Gianna looked at her, trying to figure out what was bothering her sister. "Did you two get into an argument or something?"

"No."

"Then what is it, Gemma?"

Gemma leaned against the counter giving her sister a vacant stare. "I realized I can't be with him. He told me he loves me. That he wants me, but I can't be with him."

"Why not? Because you're afraid?"

"No. I'm not afraid."

"Then, what is it?"

"I overheard Bernadette tell Mason that she didn't want her son falling for a sick woman. She said she's already had to endure one of her sons losing a woman he loved to cancer and she didn't want to go through it again."

"Bernadette said that?" Gianna asked, in disbelief. Bernadette was always warm and nice. She couldn't imagine her saying anything of that nature.

"Yeah, she did and I can't even blame her for feeling that way. Would you jump on a boat if you knew it was sinking?"

"You're not *sinking*, Gem. You're doing good. The doctor has given you a phenomenal prognosis and you literally have your whole life ahead of you."

"Yeah, well it still can't be with Royal."

"You're going to let one comment sway the way you feel for him?"

"The comment came from his mother."

"So what? You're not in love with his mother. You're in love with him."

"Yeah, so anyway, which cupcakes needs frosting first?" Gemma asked, changing the subject.

Gianna growled. "Gemma, stop being stubborn and listen."

"I've heard enough, Gianna. Besides, you want to know what the really sad part about this whole thing is?"

"What's that?"

"Royal wouldn't even know me had you and Ramsey never met. If I was anywhere else—like let's say in actual places where people meet like a bar—if he saw me in a bar with a scarf tied on my head, do you think he would've offered to buy me a drink, or at the very least, introduced himself to me?"

"Maybe."

"How 'bout *no*. He wouldn't. You know that."

"Then you can make the same argument about me and Ramsey."

"No, because Ramsey met you at your business. He brags to everybody he knows about your cupcakes and your bakery and how good you are at what you do. I don't have that. Only thing I'm good at is taking naps. I can't even drive a car without crashing into a freakin' pole—"

"Wait. What?" Gianna asked.

"Yes, I backed Royal's one-hundred-thousand-dollar Tesla into a light pole."

"What!"

"But it wasn't a big deal so don't get all—"

"What were you doing driving his car in the first place?"

"That's beside the point. Back to what we were talking about...why would a man who has the full package want a woman with nothing?" Gemma massaged her temples.

"Gem—"

"The question was rhetorical, Gianna. Now tell me, which cupcakes needed to be frosted first?"

Gianna opened her mouth to respond, but she didn't say a word. What was there to say? She wanted to be a listening ear for her sister to vent. Most times, that's what people needed – a listening ear. She definitely didn't want to say anything to further aggravate her sister. As it was, she was under enough stress. She had no intent on making it worse for her.

"The first batch is going to be chocolate so you can start on that one if you want."

"Okay," Gemma said, still irritated and weak – mentally and physically – but somehow she found the strength to pull through and take on the tasks that she knew would help her sister. And staying busy would help keep her mind off of Royal.

Chapter 28

Royal entered the fancy jewelry store on Rue de Marseille with one thing on his mind – marriage – but Regal didn't know he was along for this kind of ride.

"Ay, why'd you stop here, man? Trying to get blinged out before we hit the club?"

"I'm not going to a club, especially not with you." Royal continued on to the display case that housed exquisite diamond rings. The one that immediately caught his eye was six-thousand-dollar, French-set, eighteen carat, rose gold engagement ring. He asked the jeweler to see it.

"Whoa, wait a minute," Regal said. "Just what do you think you're doing?"

"I'm shopping for a ring. What does it look like I'm doing?"

Regal eyed up the ring and said, "That looks like an engagement ring to me."

"It is. I told you, Regal—I love Gemma. She's my *one*, and I want to make it official."

"No, no, no... this can't be happening." Regal threaded his hands behind his head and paced the floor in front of the showcase. "How in the world does my oldest and youngest brother get married in the same year?"

Royal chuckled. "I'm not married yet. She has to say yes, first."

"I'm—I'm completely at a loss for words."

"That's a first," Royal said, examining every detail of the ring. He looked up at the clerk and said, "This is the one. I need it in a six and a half."

"You know the girl's ring size, too?"

"Of course. I know everything about Gemma."

"Yeah, man, but have you seriously thought this through?" Regal asked. "This seems so sudden. Marriage is...whew—"

Royal grinned. "Why are you sweating? *I* should be the one sweating, but I'm not. You know why? Because Gemma's my *one*."

"Sir, your total comes to $6,543. We can have it ready tomorrow for an express charge of $250."

"Okay. Let's do it," Royal said, reaching into his back pocket to remove his wallet, then taking out a credit card.

"Marriage is like forever, man," Regal said. "Are you ready to be locked in with one woman for the rest of your life?"

"I am. Do you think I would buy a ring if I wasn't ready?"

"I guess not."

"And keep this quiet. I want Gemma to be totally surprised."

"Hey, you don't have to worry about me saying anything. I'll just quietly sit back and hope you change your mind."

"That's not going to happen."

Chapter 29

On Thursday when Royal couldn't take Gemma's unresponsiveness to his calls and texts, he issued her this message:

Royal: If you do not respond to this text, I'm
taking the first flight back home.
Gemma: Don't do that. I'm fine.
Royal: You're not fine. You're ignoring me and I
want to know why.

At 8:30 in the morning, Gemma was at the children's cancer center. She'd gotten Carson to drop her off for a face-to-face interview with the head of the volunteer department and while she waited, she saw the texts from Royal.

It was 2:30 in the afternoon in Paris and Royal was heading into a meeting with the third vendor he was scheduled to meet. Before the meeting started, he had to check in with his woman. Something was definitely off.

Gemma: I've been busy.
Royal: So have I, but I make time to call you.
Why can't you make time to answer the
phone?

"Hi. Are you Gemma Jacobsen?" Gemma looked up at the woman and slid her phone back into her purse, once again leaving Royal hanging. "Yes, I'm Gemma."

"I'm Ramona. Nice to meet you." She extended a hand to Gemma and Gemma accepted her handshake.

"Come on back," Ramona said.

When they were in her office and situated, Gemma began, "Um...before we get started, I have to say that I was really looking forward to being a volunteer with the children and I would still like to work with them in some capacity, but I need a job—one that actually pays. I've seen some open positions on your website and—"

"Wait—let me stop you right there, Ms. Jacobsen. I don't oversee those positions and I do believe most of them require some sort of certification which, according to your volunteer application, you don't have."

"No, I don't but there were several positions that only required a high school diploma. I do have that."

"Which position were you looking at?"

"The part-time nutrition associate position. I'll still be working with children and making money to support myself. And in addition to working, I'd be willing to volunteer for two hours a day to start out."

"But—"

"Sorry to cut you off, Ramona, but just hear me out," Gemma said. "I was ready to give up on life, and if left up to my former doctor, I'd be dead by now. Fortunately, I was surrounded by people who believed in me. People who wouldn't allow me to give up on myself. So, I didn't give up. Every day was a struggle for me, but I didn't give up. And now I'm trying to figure out my life and determine what it is I want for myself. I want to give these children hope. I want to be a positive voice for them to hold on to their dreams and their futures. Working as a nutrition associate would allow me to see and interact with them on a daily basis as well as offering my time to volunteer. And when I go to college and decide what career path I want to take, I will have some experience already under my belt. I apologize that this is out of left field, but I really would like to work here."

A smile grew on Ramona's face. "One thing I know is, people like yourself who start off as volunteers usually have a much easier time transitioning to employees, and I can tell you right off—I love your demeanor. You present yourself well—I think you would make an excellent addition to our volunteer team. As for the part-time position, here's what you need to do. Go online, apply specifically for that position and call me when it's completed. I will personally refer you to the head of that department."

Gianna smiled. "Oh my God. Thank you soo much."

"My pleasure. I will call you one day next week about the hours we need you to volunteer."

"Okay. I will have submitted the application by then. Thank you for your time today, Ramona."

"You're welcome, Ms. Jacobsen. I look forward to working with you."

Chapter 30

Royal boarded the plane at six in the evening. He'd called and texted Gemma and still, she wasn't responding. He even went so far as to call Gianna to find out what could be the cause of Gemma's sudden attitude change but even she was acting strange like she was withholding information. He couldn't take it any longer. He had to go see for himself.

Halfway through the flight, he called Ramsey.

"Royal...got good news for me?"

"Yeah, Ram. We got two new vendors. Wait until you see these products. They are of exceptional quality that I'm sure will be up to your expectations."

"Did you email them to me?"

"No. I want to show you these diagrams when I get back, and speaking of that, I'm on the way back now."

Ramsey grinned. "Couldn't stand being away from her, huh?"

"I couldn't, and then there's the fact that something's wrong."

"Something like what?"

"I can't put my finger on it. Ever since the

family dinner, she's been...different."

"That's weird. Seemed like you two were having a good time at dinner."

"We were, but then she—I don't know. Something happened."

"I'll feel Gianna out. Maybe Gemma said something to her. Gianna's sitting beside me right now with her beautiful self."

Royal smiled. "A'ight man. Later."

Chapter 31

Gemma was glad Carson could keep a secret. She'd enrolled herself in a driver's education course, but deciding it was too embarrassing to tell anyone, she told Carson to keep it between them. Plus, she had to tell him since he was her ride there.

"I don't know what you're embarrassed about, madam," Carson said. "I wish we had this luxury when I was growing up."

"So, how'd you learn how to drive?"

"My father taught me."

"Oh. I wish I had a father to teach me some things. According to my mother, my father doesn't want anything to do with me."

"Your mother sounds bitter to me."

"She is bitter. A bitter psycho. You should've heard how she was talking to me. I wish I had recorded it."

Carson chuckled. "People have their issues, madam."

"Stop calling me *madam*."

"I'm afraid I can't do that, madam."

"Why not? Because Ramsey wants you sounding like a freakin' robot?"

Carson laughed.

Gemma continued, "I'm sure he has enough money to buy a robotic butler if he wanted one. Remind him that you're human."

Coming down off of a chuckle, Carson said, "It's how I was trained. I don't call people I work for by name—at least I try not to."

"Aha! Loophole. You don't work for me."

"I feel like I do. Royal calls me so much, I may as well be your personal bodyguard."

A soft smile touched her lips.

"Is everything okay on that front?" Carson inquired. "He's been calling me for updates."

She looked at him. "And what did you tell him?"

"I told him the truth—that you've been sad ever since he left for Paris."

"Oh, no. Why'd you tell him that? Now, he's gonna worry."

Carson pulled into the parking lot of the driver school. "He won't worry if you would call and talk to him. You can't solve problems by ignoring them, Gem—I mean, madam."

"Right," Gemma said.

"Well, we're here. Go knock 'em dead."

"Thanks for the lift, Carson."

"Anytime."

* * *

Later in the evening, Gemma sat in the kitchen eating shrimp fettuccini for dinner while Gianna and Ramsey enjoyed their dinner in the dining room. While she was in driver's education class today learning about yellow road signs, she had come to a few conclusions. One – she wasn't ready to begin the process of meeting her father. One crazy parent was enough, and she didn't know what she would be getting into with Logan. Two – some things weren't meant to be – like having a relationship with her mother. Three – she loved Royal, but like her relationship with Geraldine, maybe it just wasn't meant to be. She needed time to grow and mature in order to know how to love a man. Besides didn't she risk losing a man like Royal if she didn't know how to be the woman he needed?

When the doorbell sounded, her heart sank. The last time the doorbell rang during dinner, Royal had made a surprise visit. But it couldn't be him this time, could it? He was still in Paris, right? She hoped so. Maybe it was Regal. No, Regal was in Paris, too.

When she heard Carson talking to their guest, heard the deep voice of a man even from the living room, she knew it was Royal. Her heart pounded irregularly when he stepped into the kitchen – all tall and domineering, his eyes fixed on her, seeking answers. He was dressed nice too, wearing a plain white shirt, blue jeans and a black sports coat. The hypnotic scent of his cologne grabbed her by the throat. The confusion in the depths of his eyes had her looking away from him. She couldn't even bring herself to speak.

He didn't speak. He quietly moved closer to her, pulled out the barstool next to her and sat down, looking at her. The first thing he noticed was she was wearing a scarf again, and that was possibly because she usually went to bed right after dinner and would always wear a scarf to bed – but still, she had it on and it bothered him. The second thing he peeped was something he could feel – a painful disconnect from the woman he'd given his heart to. Where was she, because this wasn't her? He didn't feel any vibes – no desire (on her end) to embrace him – welcome him back home, kiss him or show any displays of affection. She just sat there, chewing slowly, almost like she was sick to her stomach and couldn't take another bite.

"I've figured out something is wrong," Royal said. "I'm not sure what, but it's something. Talk to me, Gemma."

Gemma took a sip of water then twisted her body towards him. She knew this day was coming. She didn't expect it would be this evening, but here they were.

"Talk to me," he said in a pleading way. A loving way.

She had to disconnect from his eyes for a moment in order to find the strength to say what had been on her mind. Pulling herself together, she said, "Royal, I've had time to think about us and this relationship and I—um—I don't...I don't think it's right. I—"

"What's not right about it?" he asked.

"It's—"

"It's what, Gemma?" he asked, frowning.

"I can't be with you." She glanced up at him and saw the moment her words injured his soul.

"You can't be with me? I don't understand that. It's vague."

"It's not vague, Royal. It's how I feel."

He was frowning as he tried to make sense of what she was saying by repeating her words. "You feel like you don't want to be with me?"

"I'm sorry, Royal."

"Give me a reason."

"Royal, I—"

"Give me a reason," he repeated, his face darkening. Features disturbed. "Why do you feel you don't want me when everything—everything inside of me wants you? And where is all of this coming from? I leave for Paris and you cease communicating with me and now, you want us to be over?"

"I think it will be for the best."

"Best for who?" he said, raising his voice. "Because I thought you loved me."

"I do love you, Royal."

"Then how do you explain this?" he asked, standing.

And then Gemma forced herself to conjure up a lie to avoid telling him the truth. She placed a hand over her heart and with a tear sliding down the length of her face, she said, "I just feel in my heart that this isn't right."

Royal frowned, hurt washing over his face. He threaded his fingers behind his head and paced the floor.

"We can still be friends," she said.

"No!" he snapped. "I told you we weren't going back to being just friends, and I meant it." He paced the floor more. He knew something was wrong, but he hadn't expected this. "I—I was ready to spend the rest of my life with you, Gemma."

"Royal—"

"I was ready," he said, taking a velvet black box from his coat pocket, placing it on the table in front of her. "There's the proof."

Gemma was completely stunned as she stared at the box. She already knew what was inside.

"And now—you drop this on me?" he said, feeling his eye twitch. Feeling his heart ache. He forced back his emotions and squeezed out a reply. "You can keep it by the way, because no matter how you feel about me, I—" He stopped, took a much needed deep breath but still said throatily, "I still love you. Bye, Gemma." With that, he walked away quickly before Ramsey, who was watching him leave, could say anything to him.

Gianna, walked into the kitchen when she heard Royal leave and found Gemma sitting at the bar with her head down. She covered her mouth when she saw the black box on the table. Without saying a word, she walked over to her sister and wrapped her arms around her. She'd heard the exchange between Gemma and Royal and she knew her sister was feeling sad and weak at the moment. She also knew why, and it wasn't for the reason Gemma had told Royal.

"Come on. Let's go to your room," Gianna said, helping Gemma stand as they headed to the room.

Ramsey took the box off of the table and opened it. He hissed his frustration with the ordeal. His brother really was in love. Apparently, he had weighed all the options and possible scenarios that came with loving a woman like Gemma, and he chose her. But in a strange twist of fate, she didn't choose him.

"She doesn't want to talk about it," Gianna said, returning to the kitchen where Ramsey was.

Ramsey looked up at Gianna, still holding the ring in his hand. "He was going to propose to her."

"I know."

"What happened?"

Gianna leaned against the counter and hid her face behind her hands.

"You know something, don't you?" he asked.

Her silence told him she knew something. "Gianna, what's going on?"

"I don't want to interfere, Ramsey, and cause bigger problems."

Ramsey placed the box back on the island and said, "Gianna, my brother had a rocky past. I don't want anything or anyone throwing him back into that." He wrapped his arms around her and continued, "And I don't want you to be stressed out over whatever it is you're keeping from me."

Gianna sighed heavily. "Okay, um...at the family dinner last weekend, Gemma told me she overheard your mom telling your dad that she thought Gemma and Royal were too close and she didn't want to watch another one of her sons love a woman who was dying of cancer."

Ramsey immediately dropped his head since he knew what his mother was referring to – him and how he had to struggle through Leandra's death – his former fiancée who'd died of cancer. Surely his mother wasn't implying that Gemma would die and leave Royal in pain because it's what happened to him. "So, Gemma heard her and decided she would end her relationship with Royal to appease my mother?" Ramsey asked trying to understand Gemma's angle.

"Yes, but it goes even further than that," Gianna said. "Gemma has taken the words to heart, and she truly feels like Royal would be better off without her."

"That's where she's wrong. My brother has never bought an engagement ring in his life. I've never seen him this serious about a woman."

"And I've never seen my sister so happy," Gemma commented. "So, what do we do?"

"I'll have to talk to Royal about mother's comments. I'll keep it as plain as I can, but give him enough so he'll have no choice but to have a discussion with mother about this."

"And what about Gemma?"

Ramsey smiled. "Don't worry. Once Royal finds out the reason Gemma has been acting the way that she has, and especially after he talks to mom, Gemma's all his."

Chapter 32

Ramsey wasn't surprised to see Royal had shown up for work. Like him, his brother liked to work to get his mind off of his troubles, but after what went down last night, Ramsey wasn't sure how focused Royal would be at work.

Ramsey glanced up from the contract he was going over when he heard a tap at the door watching as Royal walked in with a portfolio in his hands – no doubt the samples from the vendors he'd visited.

"Ay, just dropped in to show you these. I was very impressed by Glasgow, but what do you think?"

Ramsey flipped through the images showcasing specific angles of buildings where Glasgow's products were being used. He nodded. "These look good. Do they have a good chunk of inventory on these products?"

"They do."

"Then I think we have a new vendor. I'll reach out to them to make it official. Nice work, man."

"Do you want to keep those or—"

"Yeah," Ramsey said, closing the portfolio.

"I'll look through them in more detail later."

"Alright, well I'll be in my office if you have any more questions. Or problems."

"I do have a question," Ramsey said. "What's going on with you and Gemma?"

"I don't want to get into it."

"It's a little too late for that. I heard you two going back and forth in the kitchen last night."

"If you heard the discussion, why are you asking what's going on like you don't know?"

Ramsey leaned back and swiveled in his chair. "Because I *don't* know. I'm not in your head, man. What I do know is, if you love someone, you fight for that person like I fought for Gianna."

"Well, Gemma told me she couldn't be with me. I'm sure you heard that much. How does a man bounce back from that?"

"Royal, this is Gemma we're talking about. You told me you loved her."

"I do love her, man. I was going to propose."

"I know. I saw the ring. It was beautiful."

Royal sat down. "I don't know what happened. I told you something was wrong. I could feel it. I didn't think it would be that though."

"What?"

"The fact that she doesn't want to be with me."

"Do you really think she would just give you the cold shoulder for no reason at all?"

"That's what she did."

"Then what if I told you she had a reason?"

"It doesn't matter, Ram."

"What if I told you Gemma overheard someone say that she wasn't right for you because of her illness?"

It seemed the blood hardened in his veins. "Somebody said that?"

"Yep."

"But Gemma's not sick anymore."

"Yeah, but I believe this person thinks there's always that possibility of the cancer returning. And since this person has already watched one of her sons live through losing a spouse to cancer, she doesn't want to see any more of her children suffer."

Royal's eyebrows raised. "These words came from mom?"

"Every word."

Royal angled his head toward the floor. He now had a better understanding of why Gemma did what she did. "It goes further than mom's comments," Royal admitted. "Now that I think about it, she was more than upset when she wrecked my car."

"Gemma wrecked your car?"

"Well, I shouldn't say *wrecked*. She backed into a pole in the parking lot at my condo."

"Why was she behind the wheel of your car to begin with?"

"Because I wanted to help her learn how to drive. You bought her a jeep and she can't even drive it."

"She'll learn. Eventually. Right now, she needs to relax. It hasn't been that long since the surgery and I know Gemma has an ambitious mind and want to do it all now that she has a brighter future, but there's no need to rush it. And I think it would be wise if you had a conversation with mom.

Royal nodded. He rolled his arm to glance at his watch. "I'm going to head over to mom's place now."

"And remember, Royal, that mom is just being mom. It's her job to want what's best for us."

"Then today, she'll know that Gemma is what's best for me."

Chapter 33

Royal greeted his mother with a hug.

"What brings you by in the middle of the day, son?" she asked as he stepped inside.

"I needed to speak to you about something."

"Okay. It must be serious, then."

"It is. Why don't you have a seat, mother?"

Bernadette sat down on the living room sofa, then glanced up at her tall son – her youngest – who looked perplexed. "You look like you have something heavy on your mind."

"I do. I need to ask you something."

"Okay."

"How you feel about Gemma?"

Bernadette frowned. "How do I feel about Gemma?"

"Yes, mother."

"I think Gemma's a good girl. She's kind. Respectful."

"But?"

Bernadette sighed. "I've noticed that you two have been spending a lot of time together lately and while she's a sweet girl, I don't think she's right for you, Royal."

"Why not? Because of her diagnosis?"

"Yes, son. She has cancer."

"No, Mom. She *had* cancer. She's cancer-free, and—"

"Yeah, but whose to say it ain't coming back," she said.

"And who's to say I won't get into another car accident tomorrow, except this time, I won't be so fortunate."

Bernadette placed a hand over her heart. She felt faint recalling how Royal was hospitalized after the car accident five years ago. "I guess you're right about that."

"Mother," Royal said, sitting next to her, "I love you dearly," he said holding her hands. "You and dad saw me through some of the most tumultuous times of my life. I love you for it, and I have the utmost respect for you. But I love Gemma, and I know in my heart that I can't be without her. I can't, mother."

Bernadette smiled, then gave her son a warm embrace. "I'm your mother and I'll always be your mother. It's my job to worry about you, son."

"I know, and I appreciate that. Some people don't have a mother to show the same loving concern you've always shown to us. Gemma doesn't have that, and neither does Gianna. That's why your words hit me so hard because I need you to be that mother figure for her in the absence of her real mother, and I'm hoping once you see how much I truly love Gemma, you'll fill that void in her life."

"I will certainly do my best." Bernadette smiled warmly at her son. "You really do love her, don't you?"

A smile brightened his face. "Yes. I do."

Chapter 34

Gianna tried coming up with a way to get her sister's mind off of Royal and a girl's dinner to South Harbor Restaurant seemed to be doing the trick. She didn't care about closing the bakery to do it either. Her sister took precedence.

"How's the soup, Gem?" Felicity asked.

"It's delicious," Gemma said, stirring it.

Felicity squeezed lemon in her tea, then stirred the ice-filled beverage with her straw. "Hey, I just realized something. We haven't been together like this since the boat party."

"Nope," Gianna said. "We've all been busy."

"Yeah, girl. I have so many clients thanks to your husband. I need to hire an assistant."

"But you already have a receptionist."

"Yes, and she's stretched thin enough as it is."

"Hey, growth is progress," Gianna said.

Gemma was still quietly eating her soup and fiddling with the necklace she wore around her neck. She'd looped the ring Royal gave her on it.

"How has the bakery been doing these last few months?" Felicity asked.

"Good. It's been consistently busy. Some days, it's been hard for me to keep up."

"Hey, on that note, Gianna, I have a confession to make," Gemma said.

"What's that?"

"I like helping you out at the bakery from time-to-time, but it's not my thing."

"I know."

Gemma's eyes brightened. "You do?"

"Yeah. I could tell, and I'm not upset about it. I want you to love what you do. Life's too short to be unhappy."

"You can say that again," Felicity said, raising her glass of tea. "That's why I had the perfect idea to help my clients find love and I'm thinking it can help me in the process."

"I'm afraid to ask what it is," Gianna said.

"Okay, picture this—a large banquet room at a hotel, completely decked out and filled with singles, champagne and fancy hors-d'oeuvres."

"Okay. I see where you're going."

"And since you already got a man, I figured Gemma could roll with me. You down, Gem?"

Gemma glanced up at Gianna and quickly returned her attention to Felicity and said, "No, I...um...I—"

"Gemma's got a man, too," Gianna blurted out.

"Say what?" Felicity said.

"Gianna, don't say that," Gemma told her.

"Well, it's true," Gianna replied.

"Yeah, but—"

"Wait," Felicity said holding up her hands. "Gemma, you got a man?"

263

"She does," Gianna said. "Gemma and Royal are an item," she told Felicity.

"We're not," Gemma said. "We broke up."

"Yeah, over some nonsense."

Felicity was still processing the fact that there was something between the two of them. "You and Royal?"

"No, Felicity. We broke up."

"But y'all had us thinking you were *just friends* and all this time you've been bumpin' and grinding?" Felicity asked.

"Ain't nobody bumpin' nothing," Gemma said.

"Yeah, but somebody gave her an engagement ring," Gianna said. "Guess who?"

Gemma glared at her sister.

Felicity's mouth fell open. "Okay...please explain to me what's going on."

"Fine since Gianna won't be quiet," Gemma said. "Royal and I became a couple about two weeks ago and he was going to ask me to marry him but I broke it off."

"Why?" Felicity asked.

"Because she's afraid of happiness," Gianna said.

"I'm not."

"Oh, yes you are. Royal has practically been in love with you from the beginning and what do you do besides pretend he's not right for you?"

"I've done no such thing. Royal is—" she paused. "Royal is everything I ever wanted, but I'm not sure I'm what *he* wants. And yes, I realize that makes me insecure, but that's what

I am, and I can't be sure of myself until I know who I am and what it is I have to offer a man. So far, that's nothing. As it stands, I can't drive, I don't have a job, I don't have a life…"

"Sounds like a bunch of excuses to me," Felicity said.

"Exactly," Gianna said.

Felicity continued, "Because if a man sees something in you that drives him to propose, then dear God why are you questioning it? Do you know how rare that is?"

"I know, Felicity. I get it, but I want him to be happy. I know what kind of man he is and I know what he deserves."

"You're not valuing yourself when you think that way, Gemma," Felicity told her. "And you have value. You don't have your own business, a job—okay, but so what? You're only twenty. Just understand that your life—your *worth* is not determined by the things you possess because some of the wealthiest people don't have value. Know why?"

"Why?"

"Because their hearts are flawed. But you, my dear, you are smart, funny, strong and beautiful."

"And Royal sees that," Gianna added.

Gemma nodded as she fiddled with the ring. Maybe she was too quick to end something with Royal before it really got started.

* * *

The women thought they were going to

finish off the night by hanging out by the lighted fire pit out back, but when Gianna pulled up in the driveway, they saw cars – Ramsey's brothers were over.

"Wait...isn't that Regal's G-Class?" Felicity asked.

"It looks like it," Gianna replied. She parked the car and the women got out, walked to the house and on into the living room toward the back patio. When Gianna opened the door, she saw Ramsey and his brothers outside by the fire pit with Carson standing at the grill. They all had beers.

"I thought you said Regal was in Paris," Felicity whispered.

"He must've come back early. Sorry," Gianna whispered back.

"You set me up!" she whispered sharply.

Gianna tried to hold in a laugh but she couldn't.

Gemma chuckled a bit, too, but the stares from Royal had the smile quickly falling off of her face.

"I didn't set you up, girl," Gianna managed to say, but she was still amused. "I didn't know he would be here. I didn't know any of his brothers would be here, actually."

"Well, hello, beautiful. Didn't think you would be back so early," Ramsey said, walking up to Gianna. He kissed her on the cheek.

"Yeah, we just went to dinner. If I knew you were going to have the crew over, we would've stayed out longer."

"I didn't know they were coming over,"

Ramsey said. "They all showed up one by one so I told Carson to throw some steaks on the grill."

"Oh."

Ramsey looked at Felicity. "Hey, Felicity. How are you?"

"I'm good," she responded. "Are you still taking care of my girl?"

"You know I am," Ramsey said, throwing an arm around Gianna. "How are you, Gemma?"

"I'm okay, Ramsey." Lie. How could she be okay with the hard stares of Royal giving her heart palpitations? "I'm going to head inside," Gemma said to escape the heat of his eyes. "Enjoy the rest of your night everybody."

"Ay, who ordered a wedding planner?" Regal asked, stepping up to the group, staring Felicity down almost like he was daring her to say a word.

Felicity was already rolling her eyes. "I'm not a wedding planner. And what are you doing here, anyway? I thought you were supposed to be in Paris."

"And how do you know that? Y'all been talking about me?"

"In your dreams," Felicity mumbled.

Regal smiled. "I'm not going to let you bother me tonight, WB."

"You—"

Gianna grabbed a hold onto Felicity's forearm to calm her down a bit and to stop her from saying whatever it was on the tip of her tongue.

"That's right, Gianna," Regal said. "Keep

your girl in check. She only hates me because she wants me."

Felicity cackled, then stopped immediately and said with a straight face, "No, it's genuine hate."

"That's what your mouth say," Regal said taking a step forward, staring at her mouth.

"Alright," Ramsey said, stopping the war of words between the two.

"Hey, Gianna," Romulus said, stepping up to them now. "How are you feeling?"

"I feel fine. Thanks for asking, Romulus."

Then came Royal. He spoke to Gianna and Felicity, then headed for the house. His woman was there and he wouldn't leave tonight without talking to her. To see where her head was at.

When he stepped into the kitchen, he saw Gianna filling a glass with water. She looked up at her bearded king, frowned a little then quickly looked away. He had on a gray sweater that emphasized his broad shoulders and a pair of distressed jeans that hung around his waist just right. On his feet, he wore a pair of brown, buckle-detailed Gucci leather boots. And she didn't know if it was because she missed him but his beard seemed fuller. Eyes darker. Lips more desirable. Dang.

"Hi, Gemma."

"Hey, Royal," she said softly. She tossed her pills inside of her mouth and chased them down with water. Then she said, "I'm surprised you have anything to say to me."

"Why wouldn't I have anything to say to

you?" he asked, leaning against the island crossing his arms, looking at her. "I mean, after all, you *are* the woman I thought I would spend the rest of my life with. The feelings I have for you won't die just because you don't want me."

His words almost knocked her off balance. "Don't say it like that."

"What? It's true, isn't it? That's why you broke up with me, correct?"

Gemma stared at him, then looked away.

"Correct?" he asked with raised brows.

"No, that's not correct."

"So you want me, then?"

She looked at him again and glanced away.

"I'm not asking you difficult questions, Gemma," he said taking slow, intimidating steps toward her.

"I do want you."

"Then, if you want me," he said stopping in front of her, "Why let other people influence the way we feel about each other?"

Gemma took another sip of water, feeling waves of body heat radiate from him.

"I came into this with my eyes wide open. I knew what I was signing up for and I made it clear to you that I loved you. That I wanted this—*us*—more than anything. But you—you've been fighting so hard against it that now, this is where we are—you holding back while I'm ready to go all in."

"But—"

"Full disclosure," he said interrupting her. "I know all about what you overheard my mother say. And you *know* my mother. She didn't

269

mean any malice toward you. She was just talking because she was legitimately worried about me, and rightly so. But I had a conversation with her about it. Know what I told her?"

Gemma's eyes teared. "What? That you love me?" she asked with a wavering voice.

"Yes. That I love you. Know what else?" he asked, placing his hand on her face, using his thumb to brush a tear away.

"What?"

He tilted her head up so she was looking at him when he said, "That I want to spend my life with you."

"And what did she say?"

"What *could* she say? This is our life to live, not hers."

"But how can we be together if your mother—"

"Skip all that," he said, interrupting her. "My mother may have played a minor role in your decision to break up with me, but it wasn't the major one. You have a lot of insecurities with yourself because you feel you're not where I am and therefore, our relationship won't work. I'm here to tell you that you have to get over it because there's no way I'm leaving you just because of some *insecurities*. I don't care about the license. The job. Baby, you can back up a thousand cars into light poles. I don't care as long as I have you."

Gianna giggled and cried at the same time. And he embraced her warmly and held her in his arms, holding her with a heart full of love.

"Now, where is that ring so I can do this properly?"

"Royal."

"Where is it?"

Gemma tugged at the necklace around her neck where she'd kept the ring since the night he left it on the table. "Here it is."

Seeing where she'd kept it only solidified their bond in his eyes. With gentle movements, he unhooked the necklace then secured the ring in his hand. It was then that he lowered himself to one knee, took her hand and said, "Gemma, this is easy for me to do because the last few days without you have been complete torture for me. I know you're the one. I knew it the moment we met. I knew it when I stayed by your side at the hospital...when I didn't even know you. And now, I want to make you mine— to show you how much I love you and make you happy for the rest of our days. Gemma Jacobsen, my diamond girl, will you marry me?"

Gemma, in full tears now, covered her mouth with her hand while he still held onto her left hand, preemptively sliding the ring onto her finger.

"Oh my God!" Gianna said, bursting through the back door like she was the law, then ran over to Gemma. "Are you guys engaged?"

"She has to say yes, first," Royal said, staring up at Gemma.

Ramsey, Regal, Romulus and Felicity stepped inside to which Ramsey said, "Gianna, baby, I think they're having a private moment.

Maybe we should all go back outside."

"No," Royal said. "Don't go outside. I want you all to witness this." He kissed Gemma's hand and stared up into her eyes when he asked again, "Gemma, will you marry me?"

Gemma sniffled and said, "Yes. I will marry you."

Royal slid the ring onto her finger and then stood up tall to leave a kiss on her lips.

"Wait. We couldn't hear that from over here," Regal said. "Was that a yes or a no?"

"She said, *yes*," Felicity told him. "I heard her loud and clear."

"Yeah, that's your job ain't it?" Regal teased. "To keep an eye out for men on their knees."

"Ugh...Gianna, I'm going to head on out," Felicity said. She couldn't take any more of Regal. "Congratulations, Gemma and Royal. I'm happy for you."

"Thank you," Royal said, and then he resumed kissing Gemma like no one was in the kitchen except the two of them.

Chapter 35

The wedding happened exactly a week later at a Lake Norman banquet hall that provided magnificent views of the lake. Even though it was officially winter in North Carolina, the temperature was a perfect seventy-two degrees. Gemma was dressed in an off-the-shoulder, tiered A-line gown with a sweeping, decent-length train. Her hair was done in beautiful curls and she wore a veil that matched her dress.

Royal wore a black tuxedo as he stood on stage with the minister, glancing over at his parents. Their example of long-standing love would surely help him in his marriage. He was sure of it and appreciated their example over the years.

He cleared his throat and watched the wedding party begin to make their way down the aisle. The men were dressed in black tuxedos. The women wore shimmery gold-fitted dresses and gold heels. Everything – their outfits, the decorations, the flower arrangements – it all looked perfect like this wedding had been planned for a year and it only took a week to pull everything off, especially with the help of Bernadette who did all the flower arrangements and decorations. She also accompanied Gemma, Felicity and Gianna to a local bridal shop where she helped Gemma find the perfect gown.

First, walking down the aisle was Romulus and Gianna...

Gemma had requested that in lieu of her father, Ramsey – the man she still credited for saving her life and giving her hope – walk her down the aisle. Therefore, Romulus stood in for Ramsey and escorted Gianna. Pregnancy had her glowing and the gold dress brought out the radiance of her skin.

"Ramsey warned me not to get too close," he whispered to Gianna as they began walking over pink rose petals.

Gianna giggled. "Whatever. You know Ramsey's only kidding around, Rom."

"No, he's not. He also told me if you trip or fall, or if *anything* happens to you or the baby, he would have my head."

Gianna could only smile although she wanted to laugh, but the guests were all staring so hard, she couldn't just burst out into laughter.

"So, pay attention so you don't trip over anything," Romulus told her.

"What am I supposed to trip over, Romulus? Rose petals?"

"I don't know. What I do know is, I value my life and I do not want Ramsey coming for me."

Next came Regal and Felicity.

"Stop holding my arm so tight," Felicity grunted. Why couldn't she walk down the aisle with one of the *normal* brothers?

"You're the one with a tourniquet around my arm," Regal said. "Nobody told you to wear those six-inch heels."

"Like I need anyone's permission," Felicity said then plastered a smile on her face.

"Well, you should've planned ahead if you wanted to be comfortable," Regal told her. "It's your own fault, Dub. Look at Gianna. She has on flats."

"And she's also pregnant, doofus. She's supposed to be wearing flats."

"If you say so."

"I'm doing this for Gemma. I'm doing this for Gemma," Felicity chanted softly.

"Don't front like you don't like being seen with ya boy."

"Oh, *puh-leese*. I'm counting the steps to the stage so you can let go of me."

"You mean so *you* can let go of *me*."

"Ugh. What-the-freak-ever. Can you just be quiet?"

"Nope. I like annoying you. You make it so easy."

Felicity glanced at him, taking in his striking good looks in the tuxedo. And he was clean shaven, smelled good, but Regal...gosh, she could choke him.

And then came the moment everyone,

especially Royal, had been waiting for – Gemma appeared, being escorted by Ramsey down the aisle while the guests rose to their feet. Some even gasped at how beautiful she was as they walked toward Royal.

"Are you ready for this?" Ramsey whispered, "Because Royal sure looks ready for you?"

Gemma looked up at Royal, then said to Ramsey, "Yes. I'm ready."

"Good," he said.

When Gemma took position next to Royal, Ramsey gave him a single nod of approval then stepped back.

Shortly thereafter, they exchanged vows, slid rings on each other's fingers and the minister announced them to the crowd as Mr. and Mrs. Royal St. Claire.

* * *

Regal kicked off the reception by popping the first bottle of champagne. "Woo!" he exclaimed when it foamed up. "Now, it's a party!"

Carson walked over to him and said, "Sir, you *do* know there are bar stations situated all around here. There's no need to pop your own bottle."

"Look-a-here, old man. This bottle right here...this is all mine," Regal said. "My lil' brother just got married. It's time to celebrate."

"Hey, I can't argue with that."

"Congratulations, Royal and Gemma," Siderra said, hugging them both at the same time.

"Thank you, Siderra," Royal told her.

Bernadette walked over and embraced Gemma warmly. "Welcome to the family, sweetheart."

"Thank you, Bernadette."

Eyes filled with tears, Gianna circled her arms around Gemma. And then she all out started crying. Like a toddler. Like a toddler who'd lost her mommy in a crowded store.

"Gianna, why are you crying so hard?" Gemma asked.

"I'm so happy for you," she said.

"Okay, but you don't have to do all this boo-who*ing*."

"I'll take care of this woman," Ramsey said, wrapping his arms around Gianna. "I hate seeing you all emotional like this."

"I know," Gianna said, pinching the corner of her eye. "I'm just so happy."

"I am, too," Gemma said.

Chapter 36

Gemma smiled. A girl couldn't ask for a better day. Perfect weather, a most perfect man and a feeling of elation – the excitement of starting a new life. Of having a new second chance. A new beginning.

Instead of driving back to Charlotte from Lake Norman since it was so late, they stayed at a fancy bed and breakfast right on the water and was sitting on the bed with a basket full of snacks. Since he was sure they would be too busy celebrating to actually eat at the reception, he prearranged for the basket to be delivered to their room.

"This strawberry jam is good, Royal. I'm glad you did this. I'd be starving right now if you hadn't."

"And you know I wouldn't let that happen," he told her, staring at her adoringly, then smiled. "When I saw you walking toward me with that beautiful gown on, I literally bit my tongue to make sure I wasn't dreaming."

"Stop it," she said, her blushed enhanced cheeks rounding.

"I kid you not. You're so beautiful Gemma."

"You're not so bad yourself, Prince Royal,"

Gemma said, finishing the last of her bread, then hopping up off of the bed.

"And that dress is amazing on you."

"Your mother helped me pick it out," Gemma said, doing a twirl in it.

Royal smiled, his eyes crinkling at the corners as he looked at her with elation. "Are you tired?"

"Tired. No way. It's my wedding night."

Royal glanced at his watch. It was 3:16 a.m. "More like wedding morning, bae." He stood up and stepped in front of her, interlocking their fingers while they swayed back and forth like they were reliving their wedding dance even though there was no music playing.

Gemma went with it, then rested her face against his chest. "Royal, this was the happiest day of my life."

"Mine, too."

"And I know I told you this a thousand times today, but I love you."

"I love you."

She smiled. "Okay, now help me get out of this dress. We have some love to make."

"Um, excuse me," he said, "But where'd my shy, innocent wife go?"

Gemma giggled. "Right here, loosening your belt."

"Alright, I warned you what would happen if you wake up the boss."

"What? He's gonna make me work overtime?"

He smiled while unzipping her dress. "Yes. Overtime." He lowered his mouth to hers, took a kiss while lowering her dress down her arms, past her waist and on down to the floor. And then, he picked her up, listening to her giggle her way to the bed where he lowered her. He removed his clothes while she watched until he was standing there, completely nude in all his glory.

Her eyes grew big. She'd seen his muscular chest before, but doggone if this beautiful man didn't have the body of perfection. The smooth caramel skin of his did something to enhance the beauty of his rigid muscles and strong, taut thighs. And her eyes nearly rolled right out of her head when she stared at 'the boss'. He was definitely large and in charge. Royal's body was so well built, it was as if someone had laid out some plans to have him designed and sculpted.

"Is something wrong?" he asked when she stared at him without so much as a blink.

"Um, yeah. You didn't tell me the boss was big enough to have his own room."

Royal looked down at himself and chuckled. Then he walked over to the bed and slowly pulled her panties down her legs, saying, "He does have his own room. He's just never been in it."

"From the looks of it, I don't think he can fit in it."

"Shh," Royal said, climbing on the bed, hovering over her and said, "Don't you worry about that. That's for me to worry about." He swooped down on her lips, kissing them and sucking on them until he felt her breaths become quicker. He lowered his mouth to her ear, feasted on her lobe and grazed his teeth across her neck, feeling her body jerk.

Using one hand, he unlatched her bra and took in the beauty of her breasts. The shape of them.

Gemma watched him as he observed her body like an exhibit.

"You have a beautiful body, Gemma," he told her. Of course, she had scars – surgery will do that to you, but those were beautiful, too.

He lowered his head to her pillowy bosom and used his tongue to tease her in a way that no one ever had. And he took his time getting acquainted with her taste – with this part of her body suckling just so before he moved to her other breast and repeated that same sensuous torture.

He growled.

"What's wrong?"

"What do you mean?" he asked, stopping to look at her.

"You just growled like..." she took a breath. "Like an angry wolf."

"More like a hungry wolf," he said, kissing a path straight down the center of her flat stomach and stuck his tongue in the concave of her navel. Her body jerked when he did it so he made sure to do it again. Over and over again.

While he paid ample attention to her navel, he used his hands to explore her what she liked to call her biscuit. Well, her biscuit was now *his* biscuit. He had a good grasp on it, giving her a firm, passionate massage there, feeling her writhe beneath him, causing a cataclysm of explosions to hit her all at once. She arched her back and moaned.

"Oh, Royal!" she exclaimed, her body trembling seemingly in an uncontrollable way.

"I love pleasing you," Royal said, watching her in the throes of ecstasy. He could see love all over her face. Hear it in her moans. "I thought I would have better control over myself, but I want you so much, I need to be inside of you. Like now."

"Okay," she said breathlessly.

Royal reached for his wallet where he took out a small, square-shaped gold package. "You keep those in your wallet?" she asked, and it's a wonder she could ask anything while she was still trying to recover from release.

He ripped open the package and asked, "Where else am I supposed to keep 'em, Gemma?"

She shrugged, watching as he sheathed himself.

"You know what...I think it'll be better if you were on top so you can control what's about to happen to your biscuit—I mean, you." A wicked, cute smile touched his lips.

She gnawed on her lip as he laid on his back, then she straddled him. "Okay, so tell me what to do first."

"Kissing me would be a good start."

"Okay, Royal." She lowered her lips to his, then moaned when she felt his large hands cup her naked bottom. It only enhanced her desire and made her want him more. "Alright. I'm ready," she said after tearing her lips away from his, coming up on her knees, taking a hold of the boss and attempting to guide him to his *room*.

"Whoa, whoa, wait, Gem."

"For what?"

"You don't know what you're doing, do you?"

"No, but I gotta learn one way or another," she said, lowering gentle pressure on him until her body slowly began to accept him. She gasped.

"What's wrong?" he asked quickly.

"It's happening!" she said in an excited, dramatic way. "Do you feel that, Royal?"

Royal laughed. "Okay, Gemma, this is not how this is supposed to go down."

Gemma let the weight of her body come down on top of him, squeezing her eyes tight while trying her best to accommodate the invasion of 'the boss'.

"Wait," Royal said, grabbing her hips, stopping her. "Don't bite off more than you can chew."

She opened her eyes, looked at him and said, "I'm fine. I'm not fragile. I'm not going to break. I finally have you—my very own husband and best friend—and I want to know what this feels like. Make love to me, Royal."

"Okay, baby," he said. Somehow, he was able to get up and switch positions with her until he was on top of her, gently lowering her to the bed again.

Gemma nibbled on her lips, anticipating what he was about to do. She could still feel their bodies connected somewhat but not fully.

She could see love, care and concern in his eyes but she could also see desire of the most potent kind building and building until he, by his own admission, couldn't handle going slow any longer, especially since she didn't want him to. And so he filled the space that separated them with one firm push until he settled deep within her soul, feeling the most intimate part of her hugging and gripping him. The immense pleasure was far beyond anything he'd ever experienced, and from the way she was panting and holding on to him, he was sure it was just as pleasurable for her after the initial sting of pain was over.

Carefully, he allowed his weight to capture her and with moist lips brushing against hers, he asked, "Are you still okay?"

"Y-ye-yes," she whispered and followed up by lifting her head from the pillow to kiss him, affirming her answer. She placed her hands on his beard, angling her head to accept his kisses, fully aware of his presence inside of her.

With the satisfaction of knowing he was pleasing her, Royal settled deeper before giving her a sensual massage. And her muscles automatically gripped him. Squeezed him – returning the favor.

"Royal." She gasped his name and when she did, he took her opened mouth as an invitation for his tongue, kissing her deeply, tangling his tongue with hers while they stayed snugly connected below. And then he began increasing his rhythms by reading her and determining what she liked while balancing what she could handle. She could definitely handle this, he thought as he listened to soft whimpers float away from her lips – a delightful noise to his ears that amplified his desire to please her. And please her he did, causing her body to jerk in a way it had never jerked before.

Gemma couldn't control the convulsions overtaking her body. All she could do was wail his name and grab sheets to confirm in her mind that she wasn't floating. And then she held on to him and cried out as those foreign sensations ripped through her body with such intensity that all she could do was hold on to him while he toppled over into a release so potent, for a few moments, it actually felt like the room was spinning. He squeezed his eyes tight and threw his head back, letting the incredible feeling overtake his being and claim everything out of him. She was taking everything.

"Gemma!"

"Oh, Royal," she uttered loudly, feeling her body jerk into another passion-induced seizure, courtesy of Royal. He had the sexiest body and all the right tools to please her with.

And it seemed that her trembling body encouraged yet another spasm as he whispered in her ear, "Oh, Gemma. This has never happened to me before, baby. You're making me...making me..." He closed his eyes and collapsed on top of her – his breathing heavy. His body shuddering – giving as she took, squeezed and wrapped her legs around him. It only drove him mad with passion – made him love her that much harder – pumped extra power into him to keep going, giving her what she wanted. What they both needed.

Love.

And they were both serving it up, neither willing to concede until they both went limp together, holding each other so tightly, it's a wonder they could breathe through the wonderful devastation of it all. Royal looked at her, and for a moment, he seemed dazed. He'd never experienced the pleasure of having his body give in multiple times, but he knew why it was happening now – because he loved this woman more than anything. She was his *one*. He knew it. The boss knew it. His body knew it and his mind was one-hundred percent in sync with knowing it. With loving her.

* * *

Later when they could both breathe normally again without it sounding forced, Royal said, "I want to know something, Gemma." He propped up on his elbow staring into her eyes as their naked, sweaty bodies rested.

"What would you like to know?" she asked.

"Was it better than the movies?"

She chuckled softly, staring into his abysmal eyes, then looking at his gorgeous, firm lips. "So much better," she said, lazily running her fingertips across the dark hair on his chest.

"How do you feel?" he asked. "You still love me?"

"Mmm hmm," she mumbled. "I do still love you, husband."

He cracked a smile, then traced her lips with his thumb. "I love you, too, wife." He smiled again. "Wow. That's going to take some getting used to—having a wife. I thought I'd be the last of the St. Claire's to get married."

"And now look at you." She reached up to run her fingers across his beard. "I would have never imagined that *we* would become *this*. I still remember the moment I was in the hospital—when I opened my eyes and saw you there beside my bed. I thought to myself, why is this extremely handsome man by my side right now when he could be doing a million other things?"

"I didn't know it at the time, but it was all because I loved you."

Her brows raised. "Even then?"

"Yes. Even then." He leaned closer to give her a kiss. "Now, go to sleep before the boss assigns you some tasks you can't quite handle."

Gemma chuckled. "You and this boss nonsense...

He smiled again. "For real though...get some sleep because I'm going to need a biscuit with my breakfast in the morning."

"Oh, jeez," she said, blushing. "Go to sleep, Royal."

"And there's rain in the forecast, too."

"Goodnight, Royal."

He grinned. "Goodnight, baby," he said, pressing his lips to her forehead.

Chapter 37

~One Month Later~

"Okay, are you ready?" Royal asked, sitting in the passenger seat of Gemma's jeep. She was in the driver's seat with her eyes closed, like she was saying a silent prayer. She'd just gotten her driver's license a few days ago and driving herself to her doctor's appointment was her first real-world test as a licensed driver.

"Gemma?"

She looked at Royal and said, "The better question is, are *you* ready? The last time you were with me in a car—"

"Gemma, baby, stop reflecting on that. That's history. My car is fixed, and it really wasn't damaged all *that* bad. Just try not to back into somebody else's car though." He attempted to stifle a grin but failed miserably.

"See, this is why you need to drive."

"Nope. You're driving. Go on and crank this baby up."

Gemma started the jeep, secured her seatbelt and put it in reverse. She checked all the mirrors and turned around as she backed out of the parking space. Once she was successfully out, she shifted the car back into drive and headed for the street.

"See. I knew you could do it. I'm proud of you, Gem. You've come a long way," Royal said.

"Yes, but I definitely wouldn't have been able to do it without you and big brother Ramsey."

"Hey, give yourself some credit, too. You're a fighter. That's why I love you."

She glanced over at him. "That's why you love me?"

"Yes."

She smiled big. With her man beside her, she was the happiest she'd ever been in life, even though some circumstances weren't ideal in other areas of her life. Like Geraldine, for instance. Geraldine hadn't bothered trying to contact her since that day she met her for lunch, and Gemma still didn't feel comfortable reaching out to her father. What she *was* comfortable with was the man sitting beside her and her new family who'd welcomed her with open arms – proof that family doesn't always have to be flesh and blood relatives. Family are the people who are there for you. People who love you and support you. Just because you share the same blood doesn't automatically means you fit that bill. Sometimes, family members fell short in that regard.

"So, what are our plans for the day again?" she asked Royal.

"When we leave the doctor, we'll stop and get a late breakfast, then I'm taking you shopping for clothes for your new job."

Gemma smiled. She liked the sound of that. She was hired for the part-time position at the hospital and would be starting in a week. Additionally, she'd be volunteering for a couple of hours a day until The Gemma Jacobsen Foundation was off the ground. Once that was underway, she'd be spending time helping with creating the foundation's mission and actively seeking patients to assist in alignment with the foundation's goals.

"Hey and don't forget we have to meet the realtor at two to close on our house."

"Our house," Gemma squealed, thinking about the last time the realtor showed them the four-bedroom house. It was only two of them, but Royal had plans to convert two of the bedrooms into his and her offices and making the other a guest bedroom.

Gemma loved the fact that they were close to the lake and right down the street from Gianna. Yep, they were moving from Charlotte to Lake Norman, something Bernadette didn't like since two of her sons were already there while she was still in Charlotte. But she knew how much this move meant to Royal and Gemma. It would provide a fresh start to their new lives together.

"It's so exciting, Royal. Gosh, I'm so happy. I never imagined that I could be this happy and in love."

Royal smiled. "Before we got married, before you even knew I was in love with you, I told you that you deserved everything good that was coming to you. Do you recall me saying that?"

"Yeah, and I thought you were crazy at the time."

"Well, this is what I meant, baby. This is the *everything that's good* and it won't stop here. My number one goal in life is to make you happy."

Gemma glanced over at him and smiled.

"Ay, keep your eyes on the road," Royal teased. "I *do* want to get to the doctor in one piece."

"Shut up, Royal," Gemma said laughing.

He leaned over and pressed his moist lips on her right cheek, looking forward to spending the day, the year – the rest of his life with his diamond girl. His wife. His *one*.

~ . ~

Reading Group Guide
ROYAL (A St. Claire Novel)

- In the outset, it's obvious that Royal has grown attached to Gemma. Does sickness bring a couple (or people in general) closer together?

- Early on, do you think Gemma has a clue how Royal feels for her?

- Do you agree with Ramsey's logic of Royal taking things slow with Gemma and being friends first? How long do you have to be friends with someone before deciding to date?

- Is Gianna too protective of her sister?

- Gianna and Carson both tell Gemma that Royal is in love with her. Do you think Gemma is so close to Royal that she can't see how he feels for her? Or is it because she automatically assumes he isn't her type?

- What were your thoughts when Royal walked into the kitchen and poured Gemma's orange juice down the drain? Is he too strict, or does concern for her well-being give him a pass?

- Do you think Royal's first time kissing Gemma too much too soon for her?

- How did you feel when Ramsey jumped to conclusions about Royal's 'late night' comment?

- Do you understand Bernadette's fears about Royal dating Gemma?

- How would you describe Geraldine? Is there any chance she could mend her relationship with her daughters?

- Discuss Geraldine and Gemma's botched lunch attempt.

  > Discussion points:
  > -Geraldine's behavior
  > -Geraldine's comments about Gemma's hair
  > -Geraldine's comments about Gemma's father

- Does not having a 'normal' mother affect Gemma's behavior?

- Do you think Royal would have shown the slightest interest in Gemma had she been a stranger on the street?

- Is it difficult to work in a professional setting with family members?

- Should you be on the same 'level' as a potential mate?

- Do you agree with Gemma's decision to hold off meeting her father?

- In what ways do Royal and Gemma make a good couple?

- What lesson did you learn from reading, ROYAL?

Thank you for reading, *Royal (St. Claire Novel)*. I truly hope you've enjoyed it. If so, please take a moment to support me and my work by:

-Writing a brief review on Amazon.
-Subscribing to my new releases email so you'll know what's coming next.
-Liking my Facebook page.
-And please visit my website:
www.tinamartin.net

Thank you for your support!

Did you miss Ramsey St. Claire and Gianna Jacobsen's story? If so, get The Boardwalk Bakery Series, consisting of the books: Baked With Love, Baked With Love 2 and Baked With Love 3.

Discover other books by Tina Martin:

The Boardwalk Bakery Romance Series
*This is a continuation series that must be read in order.

Baked With Love
Baked With Love 2
Baked With Love 3

The Marriage Chronicles
*This is a continuation series that must be read in order.

Life's A Beach

The Blackstone Family Series
*All books in this series are standalone novels and are full, complete stories. Read them in any order.

Evenings With Bryson
Leaving Barringer
Forever Us: Barringer and Calista Blackstone (A short story follow-up to *Leaving Barringer*. You must read *Leaving Barringer* before reading this short story)
The Things Everson Lost

A Lennox in Love Series
*All books in this series are standalone novellas and are full, complete stories. Read them in any order.

Claiming You
Making You My Business
Wishing That I Was Yours
Caught in the Storm with a Lennox (A Short Story Prequel to Claiming You)
Before You Say I Do

Mine By Default Mini-Series:
*This is a continuation series that must be read in order.

Been In Love With You, Book 1

When Hearts Cry, Book 2
You Belong To Me, Book 3
When I Call You Mine, Book 4
Who Do You Love?, Book 5
Forever Mine, Book 6

The Champion Brothers Series:
*All books in this series are standalone novels and are full, complete stories. Read them in any order.

His Paradise Wife
When A Champion Wants You
The Best Thing He Never Knew He Needed
Wives And Champions
The Way Champions Love

The Accidental Series:
*This is a continuation series that must be read in order.

Accidental Deception, Book 1
Accidental Heartbreak, Book 2
Accidental Lovers, Book 3
What Donovan Wants, Book 4

Dying To Love Her Series:
*This is a continuation series that must be read in order.

Dying To Love Her
Dying To Love Her 2
Dying To Love Her 3

The Alexander Series:
*Books 1-5 must be read in order. Book 6 and the spinoff book, Different Tastes, can be read in any order as a standalone.

The Millionaire's Arranged Marriage, Book 1
Watch Me Take Your Girl, Book 2
Her Premarital Ex, Book 3
The Object of His Obsession, Book 4
Dilvan's Redemption, Book 5

His Charity Challenge, Book 6 (Heshan Alexander and Charity Eason)
Different Tastes (An Alexander Spin-off novel. Tamera Alexander's Story)

Non-Series Titles:
*Individual standalone books that are not part of a series.
Secrets On Lake Drive
Can't Just Be His Friend
All Falls Down
Just Like New to the Next Man
Falling Again
Vacation Interrupted
The Crush
Wasn't Supposed To Love Her
What Wifey Wants

ABOUT THE AUTHOR

TINA MARTIN is the author of over 45 romance titles and has been writing full-time since 2013. Readers praise Tina for her strong heroes, sweet heroines and beautifully crafted stories. When she's not writing, Tina enjoys watching movies, traveling, cooking and spending time with her family. She currently resides in Charlotte, North Carolina with her husband and two children.

You can reach Tina by email at: tinamartinbooks@gmail.com or visit her website for more information at www.tinamartin.net.

Made in the USA
Columbia, SC
29 July 2019